A Place Without a Postcard

James Brush

Coyote Mercury Press
Austin, TX

A Place Without a Postcard

ISBN: 0984920528
ISBN-13: 978-0-9849205-2-5

Published by Coyote Mercury Press
Austin, TX
http://coyotemercury.com

This book was first published in paperback by iUniverse in 2003.

Cover Photo © M. Cornelius/Shutterstock

For Rachel

Prologue

On a dry and empty expanse of desert highway, two cars sat close to one another beneath a weather-beaten billboard. One of the large vertical panels had fallen in a freak windstorm that howled out of Mexico several years earlier, and no one ever cared enough, or found the billboard profitable enough, to replace the panel, just another forgotten scheme in the dilapidated west. Though a phone number stretched across the remaining panels and whispered in faded red letters, "55 -3872", a passing motorist in search of lonely ad space would have to stop his car, get out and walk under the sign in order to read the "5" that the wind had blown down.

On this day, that curious traveler would also have to look under the car that was parked over it. The car was a sporty red Acura, late eighties hatchback with not even a ding in the bright, glossy paint. An old highway patrol car huddled next to the Acura like a lonely mammal, close for warmth and company. Thin cracks snaked across the cruiser's paint. The car's owner rarely found time to clean it.

Inside the tired old patrol car, Officer Harold Benson methodically ate a large salami sandwich. Staring through his mirrored sunglasses, he paid more attention to the road than the carefully made-up woman beside him. She watched him stare at the road, tearing at his sandwich, the grease from the salad dressing glistening on his cop mustache. He was lean, middle-aged and good looking in a manly-rugged sort of way with salt and pepper hair that gave him a look of what she considered to be unearned intelligence. Obviously a gym hound, every movement was a precise flexing and unflexing of well-toned muscles. He was as bored as she.

KC smiled in spite of her agitation. She shouldn't worry, but she did. Had to. Watching him eat, her smile slipped into the concerned and tired frown she found herself wearing more and more of late. She took a nervous bite of her sandwich, and without tasting it, set it in her lap and ran her hands through the short silky blond hair that fell on each side of her thin face. She wore too much makeup as if she felt her beauty wouldn't be noticed unless she overplayed her assets but at thirty-four, she still looked youthful, occasionally even getting carded when she bought beer or a pack of cigarettes. Overall though, most of the men who woke up next to her and saw her without her artifice felt she didn't need to do much to enhance her looks, maybe just smooth out the premature crow's feet dancing near her eyes, but she covered it all up like a mask as if she was afraid she, her self, wasn't enough.

She locked her eyes on Benson, squinting just a little bit, and watched him as he watched the road, keeping the highways safe. "He's coming and he ain't gonna be too pleased. He knows about us, you know." She paused for a moment, waiting for him to respond. He turned toward her, and she watched herself struggle in the reflection of his inscrutable sunglasses. "I just don't want problems. I mean fun and games are fun an— "

"He's a trash talking loser," Benson cut her off. His bushy eyebrows made a quick appearance above his shades. "I ain't worried."

KC rolled her eyes and looked away. She might as well have been arguing with her own reflection for all the listening he seemed willing to do. She paused and began again, "You should be. He's more dangerous than you think. Bastard beat me up last week because he thought I was sleeping with the guy at the checkout counter at the grocery."

"Were you?"

"Asshole," she said. She glared at him, but it was a fair question and she knew it. She shrugged. "No, I wasn't."

Benson smiled at her, and she wondered if the smile made it behind her reflection in his sunglasses. "You know, you could just divorce him. Come in and file a police report, and you'll get everything he's got. The truck, the trailer."

KC glared at him. "The trailer's mine. Besides it ain't that easy." She looked away, staring out the window into the desert that always seemed to surround her and from which she knew there was no escape. She wanted to be somewhere that wasn't yellow. "You know that, don't you?"

The radar gun erupted in a sandstorm of digital bleeps before Benson could answer. The readout blinked "98" in bright red lines. Benson and KC looked up just in time to see a black motorcycle rocket past them on the highway, gone as fast as it had appeared, leaving behind only the dissipating echo of its engine.

"Jesus," Benson mumbled, stuffing the last bit of sandwich into his mouth. He glanced at KC, who thought he looked comically panicked, a man taking his job way too seriously. "Get out," he ordered, licking the oil from his fingers.

"Let him go."

"Wait here—I'll be back in a second."

"But—"

"This is my job." He gunned the engine of the old patrol car, already desperate to give chase. "C'mon," he pleaded with a bit more urgency in his voice, becoming just a boy itchy to go out and play cops and robbers with his buddies.

"Idiot," KC mumbled under her breath, barely enough to be heard. She knew Benson saw the word in her eyes, though. She got out of the car and with a deliberate mean-spirited slowness she locked the door, shut it and stepped aside. She barely stood away from the car before Benson gunned the engine, and the car lurched onto the road in an impressive show of squealing tires, flying rocks and dust.

KC watched his car disappear down the highway. Listened to its engine fade into the sounds of desert around her. "God dammit!" she screamed as she kicked her sneakered foot into the ground. A small piece of ancient volcanic rock lurched up from the impact of her foot and rocketed into the side of her perfect car. The rock skidded away with a metallic ding that pierced the echo of her scream and finally settled down very close to where it originally lay.

KC stooped near her car and examined the point where the rock had impacted. She touched the car with her long fingers; her polished nails—the same color as the car—examined the nick in the paint. "God dammit," she muttered, wiping hopelessly at the nick with her thumb. She added a trip to the body shop to her agenda for the afternoon.

KC looked around with disinterest and maybe a bit of disgust at her surroundings. Waiting never came easy, and the only reason she was doing it now was to make him feel bad. She would tell him her keys were in his car. She smiled when she thought how shitty he would feel. She reached into her pocket for her cigarettes and lit up. She plopped down on the hood of her car and looked at her long, perfectly tanned legs, admiring them for a moment and reflecting on how nice they looked framed by her immaculately clean white shorts and the shiny red car. She thought about her short-lived modeling career, a photo shoot in which she had posed, all leggy and high-heeled in nothing but a thong and bikini top as she pretended to wash a red car, much like this one. Her husband didn't approve, but he did buy a bunch of the posters. She took a long drag from her cigarette and exhaled into the dead air, waiting.

I

A long faint slurping sound shattered the steady hum of darkness. The thud of a bottle landing carefully on a table followed as glass met wood. Next came a thick-throated swallow and the fluttering whisper of a page turning. He listened. The sounds focused, and his fuzzy-thick mind started sorting them out, separating them from the background hiss of unconsciousness. The hum receded as he woke, but the darkness remained so long as he kept his eyes closed, which seemed like a good idea.

His whole body ached. Maybe he'd been beaten. He couldn't remember. He was lying on cloth, soft and worn, his body supported by cushions. He shifted slightly, and his fingers brushed a soft wall. Opposite the wall, his bare foot twitched in empty air. Certain he was lying on a couch, he felt more at ease.

Somewhere miles away, or perhaps right outside since the couch implied he was indoors, he heard a gust of wind pick up and drop again like wind in a movie soundtrack. A western, right before the gunfight. A whispering tumbleweed-down-a-dusty-street kind of gust. Then, following the wind, another swallow, a turn of the page, and the bottle landed again with a gentle bump as it hit the table. The animal instinct part of his brain shouted at him, panicky, that he wasn't alone, that there was someone else in this room with him. Wherever this room was.

He wrestled in the darkness, struggling to gain a hold on his anxious and questioning mind. Sluggishly, his blank mind's eye summoned strange images of deserts and speed and the cryptic warning *Don't Mess With Texas*, but he couldn't put it together, or maybe the jigsaw memory puzzle pieces weren't cut out right, couldn't be fit back together because they weren't designed to go together because design would indicate purpose and higher powers, and he was certain there were neither.

And so he must be dreaming. The thought of being suspended in a lucid dream satisfied him for a few moments as he waited for the relaxing absurdity of the dream state to carry him away with its twists and turns, ones that would relieve him of the need to feel worried about not knowing his surroundings because his surroundings were probably being conjured by his sleeping mind. He waited for something absurd that could only exist in a dream.

Sounding too concrete and too real to be much of a dream, the weight of a body shifted and a chair creaked under the weight, but no solid images penetrated the darkness, no memories came that would fit the sounds to any real room in his memory banks of recent images. Trying to remember any given place was as useless as trying to remember his name. Despite his wishes, he was locked in the here-and-now reality of waking life even if his name lay just beyond his trembling grasp.

He thought about moving, sitting up. He could ask the Stranger sitting beside him—he should know something, should be able to tell him where or who he was—but his body hurt too much, his muscles wouldn't cooperate, and it was much less painful to lie in the cool darkness a little while longer. He considered it odd that he should be so relaxed, so unworried about his inability to name himself, and yet there was a certain peacefulness there as well. A transcendence of sorts in which nothing mattered and he could relax and drift in swirling almost-images and uncolors and the foreign-familiar sounds coursing through the comfortable blanket of velvet darkness.

This must be just like death—and dread set in on the edges of the darkness like a grinning coyote lurking just beyond the glow of a campfire. He pushed the worry back into the recesses, deciding that it wasn't so bad, yet wondering if the contentment was because he had found what—*I was seeking...was I even seeking anything? I must have been...I must be*—and the Stranger shifted and turned a page—*he must be reading a book*—and he felt more alive or maybe just less alone. Even if he still couldn't name himself.

A blue thought—perhaps just the thought of blue—surged up in his mind like an explosion boiling up from under a vast sea, surging until it almost colored the darkness, but it was more a memory of color than its actual appearance, and suddenly the blue thought-memory was gone like an arc-spark flash even as he registered its existence. He waited for another flash memory or another color, some kind of pattern, but nothing happened for what seemed hours but might only have been minutes. The blue flash, the disruption of his darkness, followed by the waiting and the realization that he was waiting eagerly, fearfully, for more stimuli jarred him, and he decided it was time to open his eyes and assess the situation, to look in a mirror, to see if he could identify himself.

When he opened his eyes, he saw nothing but more darkness. He blinked, blinked again, making sure his eyes were open, and bugged his eyes out as hard as he could—*it must be dark, that's why I can't see. It's pitch black in here.* A page turned and a shiver crept down his aching (broken?) back when one obvious fact dawned on him: *the Stranger is reading so there's a light on in here.* Terror roiled like thunder on the horizon of his consciousness. The blackness no longer seemed so much like the blackness of eyelids hiding eyes. It wasn't even really black. It was nothing.

Against the protestations and arguments of screaming muscles, he forced himself to sit up on the couch. He lifted his body, pushing against gravity, trying to rise above the darkness like a man grasping for dry land as a flash flood tears over him. He fought wave after wave of nausea and drunken spinning hands that gripped and tore at him, trying to drag him into a watery oblivion. These awful hands pulled him into the blackness, and he fell a hundred soft miles back into the warmth and peace of the couch and the calm obliterating darkness where he was nowhere and nameless as a wraith.

Falling, he heard the Stranger's voice, gruff and scratchy with a vague Hispanic accent. It was a voice seldom used—almost hoarse—that said, "Hey, hombre, you shouldn't…" but the voice trailed away, fainter and fainter, "…sit up so…" and the signal dwindled, "…fast…" until he got too far out to sea to hear the transmission, and the circuit breaker in his mind tripped and everything shut off.

2

The roaring engine and now-you-see-it-now-you-don't passing of the black motorcycle interrupted the stillness of the backcountry desert highway for a fleeting instant and then was gone, its sound dwindling back to the still desert silence like the report of a deer hunter's rifle. A skinny brown coyote with spots of mange where its fur looked as if it had been chewed away emerged from behind a large yellow rock, stretched its muscles out, back legs first then forelegs, and crossed the road, tongue lolling from its dry mouth.

The owner of the motorcycle saw the coyote in his rearview mirror, fading fast. He eased his grip on the throttle, having lost interest in the sudden surge of speed, and he let the bike coast back down to the mid-eighties. He wore a pair of old jeans with the ink splotch stains of dead bugs plastered onto the knees and shins. Underarm sweat stains showed through the highway-dust coated white t-shirt. Sunlight sparkled off the rider's battered black helmet that bore a Grateful Dead sticker. Steal Your Face. He wore a backpack, and on the back of the bike where a passenger might sit, a camera bag strapped to the seat strained against the bungee cords that held it in place as its struggles, amplified by the speeding bike, attempted to throw it off.

The bike and its rider tore through the desert. The rider, glancing about, supposed it had been nearly thirty minutes since he had seen a car or truck traveling in either direction and at least fifteen minutes since the last road sign, a reflective mile marker that indicated the road was only a hundred miles old, a hundred miles since he had crossed the state line and entered Texas. He passed oil derricks, pumping the crude every few miles, continuously bobbing up and down like great metallic birds feeding while they performed their assigned task of moving the grease of ancient animals towards the gas tank in his bike. Through his helmet he could smell, sometimes almost taste, the acrid bitterness of crude that permeated the West Texas air. It had been irritating at first, but then seemed to go away. How quickly, he thought, one's senses adjust to foreign input and then just as quickly filter it out.

The rider blinked his eyes shut for a fraction of a second; it was a game he played with himself to see if when he opened them anything would have changed. It was also a dare to see how long he could go without looking or crashing. The same view greeted him outside his helmet: reddish rocky spires of mountain, cacti punctuations on the landscape, occasional desert scrub. Some of the nearby mesas themselves looked like preposterously fat, level-topped cacti with the sparse vegetation standing out as needles against the sky. Large innocuous clouds hung near the northern horizon, but the rest of the sky was white-hot as if the whole blazing sky were one immense heat generator of which the sun was only a part. The clouds had been there all day, a tease for a cool front that would never, could never, arrive. A single wispy jet trail was all that existed, all that could survive in that white expanse of visible heat. He began to sweat more when he thought about the sky, could feel the rivulets of sweat dropping out of his armpits and trickling down his sides.

To his left, an inverted funnel-shaped thing raced past. From the corner of his eye he could discern its smooth white concrete sides like a perfect Caribbean pirate house in some cool seaside island town, only this was stuck in the middle of the Texas no-man's land in the midst of lonely desert and surrounded by a barbed wire fence to keep animals away while it silently guided airplanes like an ancient buoy with a clanging bell on their journeys across the dark star-twinkling desert nights.

He reset his mental counting upon deciding that the aircraft beacon and road signs really fell into the same category, that of 'relics of civilization' or perhaps 'outposts' would be better than 'relics' as it implied civilization still existed somewhere out there beyond the next ridge of mountains, across the next expanse of yellow rock sage brush plain to places of water and trees where a person could go and disappear and forget and start over. He glanced around the desert as an uneasy feeling settled over him, a feeling of being too visible, too obvious. He looked around, an old settler crossing the desert, eyes scanning the distance for bloodthirsty Apache raiders. He imagined himself on a horse a century earlier until he understood the terror of the open on a level he had not known only minutes earlier, yet nothing but desert before and behind. He gunned the engine again racing headlong into the limbo of heat in front of him, momentarily pushing the bike up near one hundred ten miles per hour before letting it coast back to down into the cruising nineties, and having reset his mind, he let it wander as it once again explored the vast desert terrain that was fast disappearing behind him and then being replaced by more up ahead.

He felt like he wasn't moving, or if he was moving it was all going along very slowly. He glanced down from the horizon point where the lines of the highway seemed to always converge just inches ahead of the small round speedometer. The red needle wobbled around ninety-five, but his eyes told him as he looked about at the crawling scenery that he couldn't be moving more than thirty.

The rider did not notice a billboard with a missing piece of phone number on the opposite side of the highway, nor did he see two cars beneath, so lost was he in contemplation of the endless miles of perfectly straight crawling highway that lay always ahead. Because he didn't notice the billboard or the cars, he was startled to hear the faint and ghostly wailing of a police siren coming from behind him. He threw a glance into the rearview mirror just as the patrol car's reflection appeared, lights spinning and sirens blaring like some demented phantom heat mirage trying to make itself real. He glanced over his shoulder and saw it. Real enough.

He released the accelerator, and the patrol car eased up beside him. A mustached cop with mirror shades pointed angrily towards the side of the road.

The motorcycle came to a gentle stop about ten feet ahead of the old patrol car. He pushed the kickstand down, turned off the bike and removed his helmet to have a look around. He hoped for a rush of air to welcome his sweaty hair and cool him, but there was no air to speak of, just more of the still heat and the low rumble of the idling patrol car whose sides bore the words "De La Garza County Sheriff" stenciled in gold letters over an outline of Texas.

De La Garza County. That's where I must be. In a room with a couch and a chair and a reading stranger.

The patrol car's door swung open and a tall cop stepped out, rising to his full six-foot-five inch height. He approached the motorcycle bearing his clipboard, sizing up both the machine and its rider as he came closer. He stood next to the bike, looming like a living statue of the most serious cop in all the west, the image completed by the unblinking silver sunglasses. The rider looked up at his own reflection. A young, sunburned face framed by dirty brown hair, shaggy and sweaty, stared back at him with calm hazel eyes. Four-day growth was starting to look like a beard. He hadn't showered since that little hotel in Tuba City, Arizona. *Arizona? Tuba City?* Before he'd wound south for aimless days over back roads and through backcountry camps towards the western part of Texas. His eyes drifted down to the cop's name tag where the name "Benson" stood out in anonymous black against a dull silver background.

"Give over your license and proof of insurance, please," Benson said in a deliberate business-as-usual voice.

The rider reached into his back pocket and removed his wallet, an old cracked leather thing given to him by some forgotten relative for a long ago Christmas. He flipped through the wallet and removed his license and insurance paperwork. The driver's license listed him as Paul Q. Reynolds, age twenty-nine. Motorcycle class, organ donor, no sight restrictions. Paul Reynolds... Paul Reynolds... Paul Reynolds—*It seems to fit. It seems to be me*—placed the documents in Benson's waiting hand.

Benson perused the paperwork, matching the picture on the license with the face of the man before him on the bike. "Trying to free up some of your innards, son?"

"Excuse me, sir?" Paul asked as politely as he could, trying to imagine the eyes behind the silver shades to know if they were joking or mean.

"Mr. Reynolds, do you have any idea how fast you were going?" Benson asked, getting down to the business at hand.

"Sixty-five." The expected and usual lie escaped Paul's lips. The standard speeder's lie, the one that said 'Look, I wasn't paying attention, I'm sorry, it's just I've been driving a long time.' Paul didn't even think to lie, it just came out, and they both knew it was the answer Benson expected to hear.

"Try ninety-freaking-eight," Benson snapped with all the authority and law of De La Garza County looming behind his arrow-straight back. "Start payin' attention to the dial. It's what it's for."

Paul watched while Benson scribbled on his clipboard, recording the facts, transferring all the relevant information from Paul's paperwork to the Official Police Paperwork. Paul glanced up and down the highway and into the distant mesas and black mountains that hadn't left the general look of the scenery since he'd left California, since he had left once again, only this time for good, he told himself over and over again, this time to really get away and never, ever go back.

"You a long ways from San Diego." Benson observed, almost as if he could read Paul's thoughts and peer inside his mind. "Where you headed?" Benson stopped writing and looked down at Paul.

"I'm just going to visit a friend in—"

Benson began writing as soon as Paul started talking, but the moment his pen touched paper, it sprung a leak and began pouring forth its blue ink all over Benson's Official Police Paperwork, off the clipboard and onto the sizzling asphalt of the highway like drops of blood in some late-night science fiction horror flick about inhuman cops with blue blood.

Benson dropped the pen like it might explode and tried to shake the ink off his hands, but it was soaking in too fast and leaving his hands shaded beyond help. Paul couldn't help but crack a smile.

"Don't go nowhere," Benson said, stalking back to his cruiser with as much dignity as he could still spare.

Paul watched Benson storm back to his car in the rearview mirror. He opened the door and wiped his hands on a napkin, grabbed a second pen and some new paperwork, slammed the door, and hurried back to Paul. He was sweating a bit now, and his sunglasses had slipped a notch or two down his nose so he didn't look so officiously imposing anymore. In fact, he looked comical with his dripping blue hands and mirror eyes.

"Mr. Reynolds, I'm issuing you a speeding citation. Send payment to the courthouse. You have ten days. Address is on the back." Paul scrawled his signature on the appropriate line, and Benson tore the ticket out of the clipboard and gave it, along with Paul's license and insurance card, back to Paul who carefully took them from Benson's sticky blue-stained hand.

"Yessir," Paul mumbled as he looked at the ink-soaked paperwork and blue splotches on his driver's license, a blue smear over his face. He wiped it on his dead bug jeans, and Benson, to Paul's great surprise, actually mumbled an embarrassed apology about the mess on Paul's license. Paul shrugged.

"Slow it down while you're in—" but his words were cut off and drowned out by the sudden roar of a large engine, minus the muffler, screaming down the highway. The engine rumbled beneath the hood of a large heavy-duty pickup, a dually with fog lights below and deer lights bolted to the roof rack above.

Benson's face dropped and turned into a frozen blood-drained expression that Paul would never mistake as anything but confused animal terror. The truck blazed past in a streak of blue and was gone over a small ridge as fast as it had appeared. The mufflerless engine could still be heard tearing apart the afternoon sun scorched silence.

"—De La Garza County," Benson finished over his shoulder even as he turned and raced towards his car, slamming the door and tearing after the blue truck with his blue hands clutching the steering wheel, sirens screaming and blue lights spinning beneath the bleached sky.

Paul watched the car disappear. He wondered with an uneasy feeling in his stomach what would send such paranoid terror through a lawman.

He looked up and down the baked road, examined some of the spindly plants, and finally swung his leg over and stepped off the bike. He took off his backpack, opened it up and removed a couple of donuts. He wolfed down the first one in two bites, then ate the second a little more slowly as he breathed through his mouth and stared blankly at vague gray outlines representing a range of mountains off to the south.

After the second donut, dry as the desert itself, he stretched his cramped and aching limbs, twisted his body and wished for a moment that he had a car. With air conditioning. The thought evaporated like runoff in a wash, though, and he tossed the plastic wrapper the donuts had been in on the ground and walked into the desert a little ways. About a hundred feet from the road, Paul stopped in front of a deadly looking cholla cactus, unzipped his fly and relieved himself.

Paul walked back to the bike, glancing in the direction of the blazing sun still high in the white-hot furnace that was the West Texas sky. He removed a water bottle from his backpack, took a swig of water to wash down the last sweet bits of donut from his teeth, and savored the feeling the water made as it snaked down his dry throat. He looked forward to having a drink with ice in it again. It had been a few days. Paul replaced his pack, checked the camera bag to make sure it was secure, straddled the bike, and started the engine. He put the helmet on his head and glanced around at this particular lost and barren spot of land, a place he knew he'd never ever notice again. "Cops," he mumbled under his breath while giving the engine the juice.

3

A smile twitched across Paul's lips when he raced past a green and white road sign that read, "Don't Mess With Texas." The sign disappeared into the forgotten past of the desert behind him leaving only the ghost-blur afterimage of its words burned into Paul's mind. Don't Mess With Texas. Indeed. An anti-littering campaign that somehow managed to become bigger, badder, than its meaning. Like the state it announced, like the entrance to Dante's Inferno. *The state I'm in right now. The state the Stranger must live in because this must be his house.* Abandon All Hope Who Enter Here. Don't Mess With Texas. Hell. Texas. The common denominator, Paul thought, glancing down at his wind-burned, sunburned arms: hot. He remembered a line from an old movie: "If I owned Hell and Texas, I'd rent out Texas and live in Hell." Some old grizzled Adams Indian fighter, Paul mused. *The Stranger must not have air conditioning or else my memories are heating me—even the darkness sweats.*

Paul leaned a little farther forward, head moving lower, closer to the handlebars. One by one, he stretched the vertebrae in his lower spine. He dreamed of back rubs and tried to make himself feel from memory her small hands on his back, gently pushing each little bone into a "healthy alignment" while quiet music played and incense burned in some new age fantasy that was supposed to make him feel at one with whatever he wanted to feel at one with. Still, it felt good, but now she was gone. Not gone exactly, Paul reminded himself. Still out there but not with him. Paul straightened his back out again and looked in his mind for the quiet dark spot where there would be no errant thoughts, just empty space until he glanced around again and was surrounded by the West Texas backcountry: yellow, hot, cactus-ridden, crude-air-smelling, motorcycle-humming Texas.

A tall pole grew from the shimmering concrete ahead. Racing closer, the pole rose, and a sign manifested on top whispering in faded red and lonely letters, "GAS." Paul eased back on the throttle and coasted into a small parking lot adjacent to a metal building with a bullet trailer behind it. A thin black wire connected the two structures, and a wire fence surrounded the trailer. Shaved dogs, once golden, lay miserably, tongues lolling in vacant-eyed stupors, clinging to what little shade the trailer provided.

A green minivan glowed near one of the pumps. A middle-aged man leaned against it, sweaty and sunburned and staring into space while he held the trigger that pumped the gas. A woman sat in the passenger seat poring over a map, tracing a line with her finger and an intense look of concentration on her face. Four young kids sat in the back seat playing video games between blank and tired stares at the parched landscape. The plates named them Virginians.

Paul cut the engine and took off his helmet, trying to enjoy the hot but fresh air that greeted his matted helmet hair. He stepped off the bike and stood for a moment, stretching to regain his circulation then proceeded to fill the tank with super premium. He stared at a solitary oil rig across the highway, watching as it pumped crude out of the ground to be shipped to the great night-glowing refineries of the Gulf Coast and then back all the way across a million miles of Texas to be sold across the street, two hundred feet and two hundred million years from where it all started. At a buck twelve and nine-tenths per gallon, Paul was getting a good deal. Not just gas, but history and culture as well.

From the corner of his eye, Paul watched the man finish pumping, cap the tank, and walk towards the store. He nodded at Paul as he walked past with a tired half-smile. "Hot out here," he said as he went by.

Paul nodded back. He'd almost forgotten the waves of heat rising off the concrete like shock waves from a perpetual bomb exploding silently on and on beneath his feet. By this point Paul had become intimately familiar with at least thirty-four different species of hot in Texas alone. A thermometer outside the station gave the temperature: 108 degrees, record high. The pump clicked, and the minivan vacation man walked back out. "Have a good 'un," he grunted, striding past Paul.

Paul nodded and mumbled a soft, "You too," which barely croaked out of his dusty throat. Walking into the small gas station, Paul found a fairly typical desert convenience store: too much random stuff on the shelves, but not many of any one thing (except pornography and trucker speed) and none of what anyone needs. Except pornography and trucker speed.

Behind the cracked vinyl counter and the metal-racked forest of hangover remedies, vitamins and beef jerky in teriyaki, Cajun, hot 'n spicy, regular and venison, a sweaty man with curly red hair and a scraggly red beard tinged with streaks of white and clumps of dirt looked up from a girlie magazine to see Paul walk in. Paul made eye contact and then turned towards the freezers in the back of the store. An electric fan hummed. Oscillating back and forth, it strained against its screws, creating an occasional rattle in counter-point to the tired machine hum. The man behind the counter coughed and flipped a page in the magazine. Paul listened to the sound of the magazine page turn, lighter and more crinkly than a book.

Paul stood in front of the freezers, lined up beneath the glowing neon signs. He studied his choices. Finally, he opened a glass door and removed a soda, enjoying the rush of artificial cold air in his face and the thrill of cold metal as his hand grasped the can. He wanted to hold the can against his forehead, against his cheeks, maybe pour the soda over himself as in some commercial with tan bikini women on a marble beach. He glanced at the man behind the counter. Red Beard, intent on his magazine, mouthed the words as he read. Paul looked away, feeling slightly embarrassed for Red Beard but then wondering if the man was reading a serious article or perhaps some kind of letter from a college student who'd just had his first older woman.

He looked along the shelves, not so much browsing for something to buy as trying to delay the inevitable return to the motorcycle. He imagined endless miles before he finally rode out of the desert.

He walked past the newspaper rack, scanning the pornography and small town newspapers, Auto Traders, Spanish newspapers, and tabloids. A smile crept across his face when his eyes fell on one tabloid in particular— *EARTHnews*—hiding amongst the others. Paul reached down and pulled the paper from the rack. A very grainy, highly enlarged but hardly retouched, black and white image of a blurry flying saucer, caught in motion, speeding out of a thick cloudscape dominated the cover beneath a blaring headline. Under the picture in equally loud type, a caption shouted, "LATEST UFO PICS FROM AREA 51."

Clicking his tongue, Paul flipped the thin rag open to the story. Lie was more appropriate, but it didn't seem so much a lie unless one actually used words. With images it was more of a trick, an illusion. More pictures of the UFO hovering over the contrasty desert with the moody clouds punctuated the spread. One especially impressive night shot, lonely and melancholy looking, in which the flying saucer seemed to vibrate within a ring of bright lights caught Paul's eye. It looked better than he thought it would. Paul studied each image carefully, unconcerned with the text, captivated only by the images.

I have seen these lights, these blue dancing things in the desert. I have seen this picture, and I know that I have been there and these images are why I am here, why this stranger is holding me. He must blame me for putting the lights in the sky.

Paul could feel the couch pressed against his aching body. Could hear—could feel—the presence of the Stranger near him, almost as if he were hovering over him. He tried to stir, but he couldn't move. The lucid dream state was all around him; images, faded this time, danced about his perception. Though he couldn't see them so much as feel their presence, he recognized the dancing blue lights of the faded newsprint. In his mind they became more real, and then the blue thought-memory flashed again. On and then off. Paul waited for it to come again, but it wasn't coming when he wanted, only when it wanted and right now, Paul —*my name is Paul*—decided that it didn't want.

Paul listened and finally heard the faint buzz saw snoring of a large man close by. The Stranger's snores were loud and rough, and they reminded Paul of being a little boy and listening to his dad's earthshaking, house-rumbling snores bounce the walls in his room, and he remembered being a boy and playing Frisbee and tying it to a fishing rod to reel it out and pull it back in an effort to torment the dogs and with a snap (f/5.6, shutter speed 1/1000), the boy was a man photographing his contraption under southwestern skies (*not Area 51—the magazine copy is wrong, but wrong about so many things*). Paul knew the lights were real, even though the lights were attached to an old plastic disc that lived in his backpack, powered by a small nine-volt battery taped to its inside lip. The Frisbee that followed him around in his backpack earned him a living by hanging before his camera—*this is what I do*—and Paul felt the darkness close in a bit, which surprised him because he thought it would ebb as he learned things about himself. It surprised him also that he was beginning to think of the darkness as if it were alive.

Of course it didn't matter that the magazine said Area 51 when the images were made in Arizona, that quintessential desert that even stood in for Texas in certain old westerns. Besides the UFOs were as fake as the doctored image of Satan's twin daughters with the cat eyes, leopard spots, and dragon wings on page ten, but there lay the difference, Paul thought, reminding himself that the pictures were real—real pictures of a cheap plastic disc adorned with Christmas lights. The difference was that Paul took pride in his work. He was careful with the landscapes, and he always made the whole image in the camera. No retouching. No airbrush. No computer tricks and no doctor darkroom magic, only a little dodge here to darken a shadow and a little burn there to bring out the highlights. The publication of these photos would mean a decent check sitting in Paul's bank account. It meant he had a little gas money and would keep going to see any UFOs that might be lurking, ready to be photographed, amongst the trees and barrier islands of the east coast.

"Gonna read it or buy it?" Red Beard asked in a squeaky voice that surprised Paul because its high pitch seemed incongruous with the burly, rough man who sat behind it.

The man glared at Paul who stood at the rack clutching the paper. Paul folded the tabloid and walked towards the counter where Red Beard was now looking back at his magazine, which lay open on the counter.

Paul walked towards the counter and stole a glance at the magazine, laid open to a glossy photo of a young woman with frizzy blonde hair lying on a satin bed, legs spread wide, smiling while she played with her tits. Red Beard finished reading the caption. It gave the young lady's measurements as 50-24-36 (enhanced) and age as 22 (a lie). The large man looked up at Paul, marking his spot with his forefinger as he did so. Paul set the copy of *EARTHnews* and his soda on the counter.

Red Beard glanced at Paul's magazine. "Don't know how anyone can read that crap," he sneered with a nod towards Paul's tabloid. "It ain't true."

"Me either," Paul said as he laid a ten dollar bill on the counter.

"What? You ain't true, or you don't know how anyone can read that UFO crap?"

Paul smiled. "Whichever your prefer."

Red Beard gave a snort and scooped Paul's money into the register, returning two sweaty old crumpled ones and a few coins. "'Thing else?"

"No."

Red Beard nodded and looked back down at the naked magazine woman on the counter. Paul watched for a moment while Red Beard tried to read the caption on the next page. The image was of the same woman, sitting backwards in a chair, lace teddy and open crotch, with a red-nailed finger touching her smiling lips. Red Beard seemed more interested in the words that he struggled to read.

"It says, 'I'm always up for a hot night but I really like men who do it slow'," Paul read aloud, impatient.

Red Beard looked up. Displeasure showed in eyes that glared hard at Paul.

Paul smiled. "How much farther to Houston?"

Red Beard just shrugged. "Ain't ever been."

4

Paul despaired over the fact that the desert would never end. Eventually he would come to the Atlantic beach, and it would be indistinguishable from the desert that preceded it. His eyes felt heavy, and he wished he could drive in his sleep. His mind drifted towards the photos in the tabloid. They looked good. The broken landscape and the big sky. A familiar pang of regret washed over him, a wish that he had made at least one photo without his Unidentified Fake Saucer in it. One that could be just a nice landscape. He always seemed to forget to do one without the contraption. Not that he didn't like it, it was his livelihood after all, but sometimes he wanted to see his landscapes without the contraption, without any artifice, but by the time he was finished shooting, the transitory and always fleeting light conditions were no longer right. Shooting so close to sunrise and sunset or on the purple edge of fierce storms, he quickly lost the ephemeral light that made the scene work.

Paul made his living by out-shooting the other fakers. He cared how his images looked and took great care to shoot excellent landscapes. Of course this had its down side as well. He was probably good enough to get by without the UFO, selling his images for bank lobby displays and postcard companies, yet he was uneasy about turning his back on the established patterns of his life. If something worked, why upset the rhythm? He tried to think of any of the magnificent landscapes he had ever witnessed, but he couldn't remember the details of any one except through the barrel of a lens and in most cases those details centered around remembering things like f/stops and shutter speeds. Mostly so he could re-do the photos with different lenses and at different locations so he could sell more images and thus keep the throngs of conspiracy buffs happy.

Paul glanced around the steadily cruising landscape and thought about camping. He hoped to burn some film, and his legs needed to walk about. Everything looked like private land, all barbed wired in to keep people out of the great nothing. Because most of Texas was like this, Paul knew that his camping would probably have to be done illegally on some rancher's private kingdom. He tried to find a place that looked like a promising source for photographs as well as safe from zealous ranchers and small town patrolmen.

Once, long ago, Paul had had a terrible episode of self-doubt concerning his work. He sold his first images at eighteen, straight out of high school journalism, idealistic and young. He sold them as a joke to prove he could. It turned out to be better than working in a restaurant or a portrait studio or even college. The ethics or some nonsense like that bothered him occasionally, about once a year or so. His last girlfriend—Shan—convinced him he shouldn't worry. People crave fiction, she said, so there's nothing wrong with giving them what they want.

Shan sold speed to desperate fix-craving junkies and hadn't seen anything wrong with that either. Of course neither did Paul; it was more profitable than restaurants, legal retail or even college. Shan Jones. Of course that was real, not fiction, and Paul had left Shan trembling and vomiting and bleeding from her nose at an emergency clinic and never looked back. On his sweaty shaking way out, he had washed her blood and vomit off his hands in a sterile white hospital sink and had felt like Pontius Pilate as he watched Shan's blood swirl down the shiny porcelain drain, and then he walked out of the hospital and never looked back, not even to see if they had pulled her through because it had all become just too much. She could be dead for all he knew, but he didn't feel like she was. He probably would have heard, but then he did start walking wide circles around their old knot of friends. He spent more time out shooting, wandering the desert in search of the perfect lie. He took his cameras and his bags and his Frisbee shooting talent act on the road. But now his back hurt and the thought of Shan with her Swedish massage-trained back rubs made him ache even more.

Paul watched a dirty rig rumble past him, and he shuddered as the bike slogged through the truck's wake. He glanced at his speedometer. He was only doing fifty-five. He gunned the engine and tore past the truck like a rocket until it was nothing more than a rearview mirror flyspeck bobbing on the asphalt horizon line.

Paul won a junior high science fair with a Frisbee and a point-and-shoot camera by making an image of a UFO in his yard. Years later, his job was just a refined version of the same science fair practical joke, which for him had proven to be so much more practical than simply making a volcano out of papier-mâché and baking soda that would boil out red food-colored lava. His project became his career more by accident than any real and logical choice, like everybody else set in ways they never imagined when they were teenagers. A life chosen for expedience, it seemed to him. He just followed his natural talents and inclinations. Paul wondered at the idea that perhaps he really hadn't progressed in any way since seventh grade except that now he knew how to shoot and force perspective. How to use the hyperfocal distances so that his images seemed natural, and most importantly real enough to dwell on the pages of the tabloids and yet fake enough to allow a sense of accomplishment at having been able to do such a damn good fake. His images looked just like real UFOs. Paul knew this for sure because he was the maker of the UFOs, one of the best in the business, according to Buddy Fielding, editor-in-chief of *EARTHnews* in Houston. Paul intended to stop in and meet Fielding.

Never overly interested in UFOs, Paul had always known there was nothing to it and never would be until he saw the proof of it with his own eyes. That was, after all, the test of truth. Since he was in the business of manufacturing proof of the unreal, he had become very, very certain that there was nothing out there beyond himself and this lonely desert. The truck disappearing from the rearview was real. The cacti strewn desert was real. The hum of the bike was real. Red Beard was real, but the cleavage of the magazine woman was fake—a darkroom technique. The UFO was real, but it was a real Frisbee. Not a real UFO.

The Stranger is real. I think. The blue light is not real. I do not see lights. I create the lights—they can't be real.

The Stranger snored. Paul felt himself sweating, felt his chest tighten, and he began to wonder whether or not he was paralyzed, but he twitched his toes and felt the pain, which was real. The blackness was real too and the breathing and the Spanglish stranger, but the motorcycle ride in the desert may have been real but was not what was happening now, rather it was some seductive memory that wanted to seem real. It would be happy to take him away forever through the desert to the Atlantic beaches if he only let it. He decided that he needed to try to get up again. Ask the Stranger where his motorcycle was and why he was in so much pain and why for all his memories he still couldn't remember where the hell *I am*.

Sounds grew more distinct, more recognizable, as Paul accustomed himself to the numbing pain of his body and the absence of light and the Stranger lurking somewhere beyond his memory, deep in the interstellar blackness. Except interstellar blackness was full of hydrogen and Paul's blackness was full of nothing save breath and pages turning like the fluttering wings of birds beyond a windowpane. He was certain he'd been on a motorcycle, his beautiful old bike, not a crotch-rocket sports machine, rather a serious bike. He was pretty certain it was gone now, totaled in some kind of accident. He remembered laying his first bike down as a teenager and having to limp home, bloody and sore with pride wounded more than body. This was similar but worse. Bigger. What puzzled him, what scared him more than even being a vegetable in a hospital ward with his gloomy-faced mother peering sadly down at him and what kept him from leaping up to ask a bunch of questions, assuming he could leap up, was the certain fact, the absolute knowing, that he was not in a hospital.

He didn't open his eyes, lest the Stranger might be watching and anyway it still seemed like an impossible task. Too much movement. He felt nauseous and sick and unbelievably hungry as if he hadn't eaten in several days. He listened to the darkness for a while, picking out isolated sounds, creating an aural image, a surround-sound picture of his space, and he noticed a difference. His hearing was more acute. This was why he knew he wasn't in a hospital: he couldn't hear the electricity. When he had been with Shan in the emergency room, he'd heard footsteps. Confusion. Metal objects dropping on tile floors and hospital paging systems and pained breathing, moans, swearing, crying, praying, and police radios. Here, in this dark place where blackness had learned to be a sound, there was nothing. Except the Stranger and the wind that blew against the walls separating the indoor and outdoor universes. The wind sounded distant, thwarted and lonely.

He and the Stranger were inside a room with no electricity. The lack of electricity buoyed Paul's hopes for a few countless moments because he decided it must be a good sign not to be on a life support machine, but then the darkness closed a bit, becoming tighter and constricting the hope like a preternatural python feeding on fear strangled from its victims as Paul wondered if he might be in a morgue. No, he thought, pushing the slippery thought from his mind, a morgue would have to have air conditioning.

Even a small town backwater morgue? Yes, he decided, otherwise the corpses would fester and that would probably violate some state code. Besides, he was on a couch.

The python eased its grip on the hope, and Paul wondered why his subconscious had chosen to animalize the dark, but not the hope. He thought of lying in a morgue, with no air conditioning as a large blue python slowly wrapped itself around him. He imagined the tentacles—*pythons don't have tentacles... they are a great tentacle*—and Paul knew he was still in a quasi-dream state, but the realization of his phantastic errors and his corrections, the editing of his dream work, made him realize he must be approaching lucidity. He decided, more firmly this time, that if he could still think and to an extent reason and especially feel pain, he must not—could not—be dead.

The snoring stopped in a confused and strangled intake of breath—the Stranger probably did not realize he was asleep. A chair creaked as it gave up its weight, and the Stranger's footsteps padded past Paul's center of consciousness. The universe expanded, growing in waves of noise that surrounded the Stranger's movements. A cabinet opened and closed—wood on wood—and then a can popped, and the Stranger took a sip. Paul listened, but all he heard was the Stranger's breath alternating with the occasional slurp from the can. It sounded different to Paul, sloppier, than the earlier drinking that must have come from a glass, and Paul remembered the sound of the glass being set on the wooden table and the sound of pages flipping, and the image that formed from his memories of old movies was that of a guard. He wondered again why he wasn't in a hospital. Why, since he had obviously been in and survived (he hoped) a wreck, was he in a place with no electricity and nobody save the patiently waiting Stranger? Paul listened for more movement and upon realizing there was none began to understand that the Stranger wasn't so much guarding him as watching him, probably out of curiosity rather than duty.

"Take the blindfold off," Paul blurted suddenly. The words tripped clumsily from his mumbling lips, his raspy voice cracking in his throat. He thought he said it perfectly, but listening to the words whisper from his lips, he realized it had been a very long while since he'd spoken. The blue flash-memory went off across his brain, between his eyes. An ice pick migraine erupted in his brain. "Take it off," he said again, a bit louder and with more clarity. He tried to ignore the ice pick twisting in his head.

Footsteps and the Stranger's breath approached him. The air around Paul moved. He smelled beer on the Stranger's breath. A slight breeze stirred. He felt the Stranger lean over him on the couch. A gentle laugh wafted down from above him, shimmering through the darkness. "You ain't wearing no blindfold," the voice said. The Stranger's voice with its gruff Hispanic notes sounded strangely polite and betrayed concern. Almost.

Paul popped his eyes open. He reached up with sore aching muscles until his raw fingers touched his eyelids. Arms and shoulders weakly protested the sudden movement. He held his lids open, but he was too weak to apply much force. They felt open. He touched an eyeball, delicately, with the tip of a finger and the salty rush of his dirty fingertip on the cornea thrilled the zillions of little nerve endings in his eye. From his optic nerve to his brain one signal went through loud and clear: malfunction. Paul tried to roll over, to lie more on his back than on his side. He wanted to face the Stranger. Was he above him, up in the deep space darkness? His pulse quickened, and he drew in a sharp breath. He still held one eye open.

"Is it open?" he asked. "It's open, right? Shit!" Paul let go, and his eye blinked, trying to remoisten itself. He let his hand fall to his chest.

The Stranger's breath came closer again and the smell of stale beer upped Paul's nausea a notch and momentarily stole away the hunger. Paul felt as if a great drunken dog was sniffing him. *Dogs see with their noses. I wonder what the Stranger sees.*

"Yeah, man. You got your eyes open all right," came the Stranger's pronouncement, calm and matter-of-fact.

"This isn't a hospital." Paul waited for a response from the darkness. It seemed to take forever. Was the Stranger still looming above him? Or had he moved? Which way was up? The Stranger shuffled and took another noisy sip of his beer. "Why didn't you take me to a hospital?" Paul asked. Even the darkness was sweating, vibrating with Paul's near panic fear. "I crashed my bike—I must have. Why am I here? Where is here anyway?" Paul waited for a moment. Nothing. More seconds (minutes? hours?) passed while Paul's mind raced through the rubble of his shattered memories. The blue spark flashed, burning Paul's brain and leaving an afterglow that lingered but then was gone as if remembering made him forget to watch the spark. "Talk to me," Paul shouted, slamming his fist into the soft back of the couch. Even this hurt.

"I didn't think it would be a good idea. To take you to a hospital," the Stranger's voice ebbed through the darkness. It seemed to glow like a dark beacon leading farther away from visible light, a strange radio sun. It was the only way Paul could discern up from down. He felt himself shaking, but the darkness all around didn't give or dissipate.

Somewhere, the python slithered through the black world beyond the Stranger, but closer than Paul liked.

5

After straddling the motorcycle all day, Paul's legs rejoiced to work out the kinks on a short hike around the base of a rugged mountain that formed the centerpiece of De La Garza County Park. Four dollars admission fee and no highway motel could best the starry desert view as soon as the sun went down. Paul scanned the scenery as he paced over broken ground. The sun hung low over the horizon, already beginning its quick slide below the land. Paul wanted to squeeze off a few shots before the sky grew too dark to work. The bulky camera bag dug into his shoulder, and he constantly had to shrug it up higher and higher towards his neck, never finding a comfortable position.

The park itself was simple. Completely primitive camping—no amenities of any kind and far off the retired mobile home circuit. Paul really longed to be back at his campsite, which consisted of a cheap little trail tent and his motorcycle. He saw himself with legs outstretched, relaxing by a fire, but he felt obligated to look about the park first, scouting for a salable image. Besides his legs needed a walk.

He scrambled over a large outcropping of rock and surveyed the area from the higher vantage point where he could see the washes and gullies inscribed on the land by floodwaters. Paul had once seen dry desert turned in an instant to boiling river on a camping trip many years ago. He was just high enough to watch it race by in a canyon he was camped above. He would never forget the noise and the animal terror that told him to flee despite the fact that he knew he was safe above the violence of the water as it washed dead trees and animals to some unknown destination.

He studied the sky for a few moments, judging the light while a small group of turkey vultures circled ever upward on invisible thermals, spiraling up the sky only to glide back down and ride the elevator up again. Paul's gaze slid back to the broken and unimpressive desert that rolled out in every direction. Distant mountains shimmered in the heat of late day, eager to throw their burden of temperature away as soon as the sun left them.

Below his feet, a twisted pile of rocks, balanced precariously one atop the other by eons of flood and wind, called for his attention. Paul scrambled down the other side of the rock ledge, cursing every time his camera bag banged against the rock. He wondered why camera bags weren't made as backpacks and filed the idea away in case he should ever want to invent something. When he got to the base of the sculpture, he realized it was about as precarious as the Empire State Building. It was in fact a single rock, solid and eroded into an impossible Dr. Seuss cartoon form.

Behind the rock formation, the sun hovered a few short degrees above the horizon, the eastern sky already fading into purple. The sun glowed dim orange through thick summer air. Paul knew the light he wanted would appear in five more minutes and only last for three. He set his camera bag down and started framing the image in his mind. He watched the sun descend, seeing it in black-and-white in the rectangular shadow box of his camera. His hands, of their own volition, removed the camera and attached a 25mm lens. His hands built the camera while his mind created the image. He reframed the image, compressing it to enlarge the rock form. He unscrewed the lens and attached a 35mm. Not much change, but enough. He imagined low twilit clouds, bottom lit from the sun, which would be only a few degrees below the horizon.

One more minute, Paul thought, mentally ticking away the seconds. He set the camera down and extended the tripod. He attached the camera and pointed it out at the desert. He adjusted the frame and focused the lens on an imaginary point ten feet away. He was close enough to the formation that he knew it would blur slightly as if the hurried photographer were hiding behind it, but enough of its form would be visible for one to appreciate its structure. He took a last look through the viewfinder and adjusted one leg of the tripod, lowering it slightly. He set his shutter speed and f-stop and glanced over at the sun in time to see the last sliver of it disappear beneath the earth.

With his mental clock ticking like a time bomb, he dug his Frisbee from the camera bag. Several layers of tin foil coated it, and every few inches around the circumference, Christmas lights protruded. Paul inserted a nine-volt battery into a clasp on the underside of the disc, and the lights came on. They glowed dimly beneath the coat of frost he had applied to soften them. A long strand of dental floss hung from the side of the Frisbee opposite the battery. The string was exactly thirteen feet long.

Paul grasped the end of the floss string in one hand and the camera's cable release in the other. He hurled the Frisbee out in front of the camera. Its weighted and wobbly flight arced upward. Then, as it crossed the axis of the camera lens, Paul gave an expert yank on the floss and simultaneously pressed the shutter release. The camera clicked, and the Frisbee crashed to the ground.

With time for one more shot, Paul ran to the Frisbee hoping he wouldn't need to change any of the lights. He kept a box of spares frosted and ready to go, but he had left them in his auxiliary bag back on the bike. He picked up the Frisbee, saw that all the lights were still on, and scrambled back to the camera. He opened the aperture a little bit to compensate for the fading light, took the same position one foot to the right of the camera, and tossed the Frisbee out again.

As the Frisbee sailed through its uncertain flight, Paul wished he had the time to snap one more image. One without the Frisbee. It might make a nice postcard to sell at the ramshackle gift shop at the park entrance. He smiled at the idea of being a postcard photographer, but as he yanked the floss string and released the shutter, he knew he would have to seriously scale back his standard of living. Probably sell his bike. He could do both of course, but he knew that if he used his finest images for the tabloids, they would fetch substantially more money.

Paul finished his nightly ritual of cleaning the cameras and lenses. He cleaned everything, whether or not he used it, partly because highway dust managed to find its way to anything of value and partly to pass the hours before his body told him it was time for sleep. He tucked the camera body and lenses back into his bag and sealed it up. Nearby, his fire crackled and glowed orange in the perfect desert night. He watched as the millions of tiny sparks, luminous insects migrating home, floated up into the stars, and he stared for a few moments, hoping to catch a glimpse of a satellite as it tore across the sky from horizon to horizon in a matter of seconds. He waited, but the sparks hid any satellites that might have gone past.

Paul dug into his backpack and removed the speeding ticket. He had no intention of ever being back in Texas and certainly not in De La Garza County. No intention of ever paying the fine. He held the yellow slip of paper over the fire and dropped it in. The flames caught the paper, and the sides curled in black waves. Paul watched the paper's mass drift away as smoke until all that was left was an ashen ghost of the yellow envelope-ticket.

He tried to imagine the great barrier islands on the Carolina coast. To imagine himself living in New England. Maine, perhaps. Paul wanted to live by the sea, but he wanted to live by a cold and hard sea with mountains nearby. Not the sun happy, easy coast of California. He yearned for the solitude of a place no one wanted to spend vacation time. Hell, he thought, they could see UFOs up there.

He removed the tabloid from his pack and stared at the cover. No byline hung beneath the photo. It was completely anonymous. Caught by a random guy with a camera. A guy who could shoot. Paul grabbed his old Swiss Army knife from his pocket, opened the scissors, and cut the picture out of the tabloid.

From his bag, Paul removed a roll of scotch tape and an old spiral notebook with a glossy blue cover. Paul opened it and flipped almost all the way through to find an empty page. There he taped the photo from the tabloid, and underneath he signed his name followed by the notation: "Monument Valley, AZ." He did the same with all his other pictures from that issue. The notebook, fat with taped images, was almost full, and he wondered whether he should quit when he reached the last page.

He stared at the image, barely discernible in the dancing light of the small scrub wood fire. He leafed lazily through the notebook, letting other images of other UFO sightings flicker across his vision. Happy memories of other nights alone in the desert drifted through his mind like the flames of countless campfires. Every night like every other. Always the same craft. Always the same Frisbee. Paul closed the notebook and replaced it in his bag. He did not mind this part of his life; it was the other part—the city part. The California part. He tossed the tabloid into the fire and watched the flames flicker like a nova for a few seconds while they consumed the magazine and eventually returned to their dwindling glow.

Paul dug a joint out of his pocket. He rolled it before he ate, and now it was time to unwind and drift away from the day and into the next one. He lit the jay off a twig plucked from the fire and savored a long drag. He exhaled, letting the smoke from his lungs rise into space with the smoke from the fire. Paul leaned back and studied the stars while he got high and drifted off to sleep beneath those same unfathomable southwestern desert stars.

6

The sun, fat and heavy, hung above the darkening horizon. The lamp on Paul's bike blazed through the indigo streaks in the sky like a Japanese lantern. A fast Japanese lantern. He'd spent most of the day off his bike, exploring the park but not finding any useful lighting, so the cameras stayed in their bags while he wandered the piece of desert owned by De La Garza County until he knew every stand of prickly pear. It was almost evening before he left, and now Paul felt low empty rumblings in the pit of his stomach cramping into a tight hunger pain that shot up into his chest.

Just outside the park, a green town sign had located the county seat: "ARMBISTER 30 MILES." Paul reckoned the sign disappeared behind him twenty minutes earlier, so he figured he would be getting into town soon. As the thought crossed his brain, he streaked past another green sign reflecting bright and eloquent against the purple eastern horizon: "ARMBISTER CITY LIMITS. POP. 693." Six-ninety-four, Paul thought, entering the so-called city.

He slowed his bike hard. A sign boasted that speed was strictly enforced by radar, so Paul eased down to the required forty-five and coasted along the small town's main drag.

Armbister had already shut down for the night. Paul rode through, barely registering the forgotten glass-fronted hardware stores, the breakfast cafe, the feed store in the old Quonset hut, the darkened police station, and the combination dog grooming/adult video operation. Paul's eyes lazed back and forth behind his smudged visor searching for signs of life like an astronaut exploring some alien world.

Paul passed an elderly couple driving the other way, poking along in an old yellow pickup truck with two large dogs standing in the back, noses extended into the sensory rush of automobile wind-chill. The larger dog, a Rottweiler, stood with his massive paws on the gate. Halfway through town, Paul passed a small knot of teenagers. The boys wore cowboy hats and the girls tight-fitting jeans in primary colors. They stood outside the Dairy Queen, bumming smokes off one another and waiting for something to happen. They glanced up as one to watch Paul slide past then, all interest lost, went back to their own conversations.

Two cross streets and one junction for another highway created the basis for Armbister's grid. It seemed slightly larger than many of the small highway towns Paul had traversed, towns whose economies were geared around providing food to high school students on lunch and issuing traffic tickets to passersby. Armbister looked like most of the towns Paul crossed since leaving home. Funny thing about home was Paul never felt at home there. Not that he felt at home on the road or anything romantic like that, but when he was on the road he didn't notice the lack of a place to which he should feel rooted. Eventually the lack of stability began to feel very, very stable, and he quit thinking about home altogether, either as a place or an idea. For now, Armbister was home. After dinner, it would be forgotten.

On the east side of Armbister, a blue neon sign atop a white concrete building lit up for the night like an incandescent explosion as unknown fingers flicked a secret switch. "Ernie's Joint," the sign read, but the "t" flickered as if the neon in that particular tube was nearly exhausted and had to struggle mightily to get itself lit. The hunger in the pit of Paul's stomach lit up too, and the meaning of the sign skipped over his higher brain and went straight to the hungry reptilian part. The hunger flickered on and off with the fast approaching "t" until the light came on, and the hunger stayed too.

Darkness held most of the sky, and Paul could see Vega high in the northeast. Deciding it was dinnertime, Paul eased the throttle and coasted the bike into Ernie's parking lot. He parked close to the door, next to a large blue dually decked out in unnecessary lights. He killed the engine and removed his helmet, the now-almost-cool desert night washing over him like water. He stepped off the bike and glanced around at the other cars. Three pickup trucks and a decrepit semi sat in the parking lot. One of the trucks was the dually and another was probably built in the 1940's. The dually looked fairly new, blue and spotless, it must have been someone's pride and joy. The third pickup, a Ford, bore a sticker of a popular cartoon character pissing on the Chevy logo, and all but hidden on the bumper, beneath a layer of dirt, Paul could make out a confederate flag. Next to that, a sticker of the Texas flag with the word "SECEDE" printed over it made Paul smile. Fuzzy dice hung on the rearview mirror behind a small green odor-killing tree.

Paul stepped to the wooden door and pushed it open. He strode into the bright fluorescent room. Country music drifted out of a jukebox on the far wall; slide guitars and big-hat crooning soared off the walls and around the patrons. Three men at a table simultaneously looked up as he walked in. One of the men, an enormous ponytailed man sweating with the effort of breathing, gave an indifferent nod in Paul's direction then turned his attention back to his table mates. His short arms seemed to rest on his sides, and Paul wondered if they ever hung straight down or if they were permanently half-extended in that weird birdlike manner.

A very skinny, mousy-looking man sat at the table with the ponytailed man. His long, stringy hair framed a moon-cratered face that needed a shave almost as bad as Paul. His dirty cap read, "John Deere" in bold letters. The third was an intense looking man with a broken nose and a flannel shirt. Next to Pony Tail and J. Deere, Broken Nose looked downright GQ. All three looked as if they had spent a long day working hard in the sun.

Paul returned Pony Tail's nod and walked past the table towards the scratched up chrome bar behind which a sweaty man who looked like he'd lost more teeth than he could remember stood staring blankly up at the muted TV hanging above the griddle. The TV seemed less like a window to the outside world than an eye of the outside world, peering in at this forgotten realm. Beads of sweat stood out on the cook's face, and a burning cigarette dangled from his lips.

"What do you want?" the man, whose name tag read "ERNIE," asked as he turned from the TV to look at Paul. He watched as Paul set his backpack on the counter and stole a glance at the red menu above the bar.

"Burger, fries, and a soda," Paul said, not really reading the menu since he already knew what he wanted.

Ernie nodded and snatched a green plastic cup, looking a little chewed, from under the counter. Paul's mouth grew drier and drier until a dust devil rose off his tongue and flew down his throat, his body temperature rising as he watched like a starved dog while Ernie—*faster*—filled the cup with ice and pushed it against the plastic lever on the soda fountain. Ernie stared at a weather map on the silent TV. The staticy map disappeared, replaced by a graph showing the day's highs and lows: 109 and 90.

"Damn scorcher," one of the men complained.

"Food'll be out presently," Ernie said, setting the icy soda in front of Paul.

Paul lifted the cup to his lips, sipped, and felt as if he were diving into a cool stream. He took another drink and let a few chunks of ice slide into his mouth and melt on his tongue. Paul studied Ernie while he flipped the burger on the steaming griddle, never taking his eyes from the TV. The meat sizzled and steamed on the slick black surface of the griddle, and the sharp odor of seared meat and black pepper reached Paul's nostrils, managing to overpower the ambient cigarette smoke. From behind Paul, a deep voice erupted out of the whispers of conversation. The voice belonged to Pony Tail. "Aw, shit, man, don't go back to Houston."

"I miss my boys," J. Deere said.

Paul listened, realizing it had been days since he'd heard conversation, much less participated in one. "City's so damn crowded, though, now," J. Deere added.

A sizzle erupted on the flat top as Ernie pressed the spatula hard onto the burger. The TV showed a team of paramedics loading a stretcher into an ambulance. A blood-soaked sheet hung over the stretcher.

"You're just better off you're gone now." Broken Nose's two cents.

Never batting an eye from the TV, Ernie flipped the burger and ashed his stumpy cigarette over the floor.

"Thank God, fer bein' single and rootless. I ain't gotta answer up to nobody. Not like you guys," Pony Tail all but shouted with manly delight. "You sons of bitches are whipped."

"I'm not—"

"—You did, so you's tainted," Pony Tail jumped in again, cutting off J. Deere, as if his rebuttal were pre-scripted. "I, however, maintain the purity of my independence."

An old photo of a police officer appeared on the television screen with the caption "Harold Benson" beneath it. Still watching the TV like a guardian of scanlines, Ernie, with practiced dexterity, scooped Paul's burger onto a grocery store bun on a white plate. An obligatory piece of lettuce, onion slice, and a mealy looking piece of tomato lay unhappily next to the burger.

Broken Nose spoke up loud, "You're just sayin' you ain't never got laid and trying to make it sound all special like some church girl sayin' her virginity is a gift to her future husband."

J. Deere erupted in squeaky laughter, and Ernie cracked a painful, toothless smile. Even Paul, now trying a little too obviously to listen without drawing attention, began to smile until he glanced from his burger up to the television window-eye and saw something that his mind just couldn't process for the first few seconds he stared at it.

A picture of a man's face.

A picture of his face.

A picture of Paul Reynolds.

When he realized he was looking at himself, the laughter stopped. Everyone else saw him too. Saw his face up there above the grill. A blowup of the California driver's license that had been pulled out of some database. The face, a few years younger, more innocent and clean-shaven, belonged to him. Everyone in Ernie's Joint, staring the outside world in its eye, knew that the focus of its attention was sitting at Ernie's bar with a half-eaten burger.

Paul swallowed and set his burger on the plate. He felt the eyes of all four men shift with an audible Batman-swish pan from the TV set to him. He glanced at Ernie who took an uncomfortable step back to size him up and weigh him like a hunk of ground beef. Paul glanced behind him and looked into the glittering eyes of the rough men at his back. Predator eyes. They all watched, not so much angry or scared, but curious about what might happen next. Broken Nose seemed to be fighting back a gleeful smile. One of the men farted.

"You got pulled over by that cop yesterday?" Ernie said softly. "Some terrible business, that."

Paul turned back to face his accuser. "Yeah, but–"

"Seems yer wanted for questions."

Paul stole a glance at his backpack lying on the counter. He made a quick inventory of its contents, mentally tallying the items: small pipe, baggie full of weed rolled up in a t-shirt near the bottom. He fidgeted—not too much weed, but there couldn't be any talking to cops, couldn't be any straightening out this mess, until he had a chance to dump, but then no weed, and Paul didn't want that. It wasn't much, he rationalized. But it was enough. He treasured his fireside smokes as he sat under the stars each night. He contemplated life without that pleasure and decided it wasn't an option. Better to run. He hadn't killed anyone. *It'll sort itself out.*

"Got the wrong guy," Paul said with more confidence than he felt.

"Old Harold was a good customer. Come in every Wednesday." Ernie slid his hand under the counter and removed a sawed-off shotgun. "Sure looks a hell of a lot like you. On the teevee."

"Seems they wanna talk to you," Broken Nose said. "Like maybe you was the last person that seen him alive." He nodded slowly.

"Well, shit, kid," J. Deere squeaked.

Paul glanced from one to the other, then back to Ernie.

Pony Tail leaned back in his chair causing a great creaking sound to vibrate through the diner. "You know," he began slowly in a John Wayne drawl, "folks don't have much reason just to pass through here—unlessen they're hidin' or not wantin' to be noticed or sumptin." All the men laughed at Pony Tail's impersonation. Even Pony Tail seemed to be amused by his own humor. Through building laughter, he managed to add, "Pilgrim."

Paul glanced back at his pack, double-checking his options, but this time Ernie caught the look.

"What's in the pack?" Ernie demanded.

"Head of a too-damn-nosy cop," Paul shot back without thinking and immediately wished he could retract his words.

The men at the table laughed, as if in admiration of Paul's doomed bravado. Ernie simply hefted the shotgun and leveled it at Paul's chest. "Get out," he growled.

Paul rose to his feet, picked up his camera bag, strapped on his backpack. Reached into his pocket and removed the bills Red Beard had given him and set them on the counter in a neat pile. Without taking his eyes from Ernie, who was already counting the money, Paul carefully backed past the round table, towards the door.

"Why, Ernie," Broken Nose said, "You gonna let him just escape? You could be a regular god damned hero. Get him!"

"Shut up, Joey," Ernie snarled at the broken-nosed man. Ernie switched his glare to Paul—venomous rage glowed in his dull eyes, and a wicked smile crept across his sweaty face. "And he's a dollar shy." He hustled around the counter. "That's theft of service," Ernie yelled, chasing Paul from the restaurant and brandishing the shotgun. Joey and the other men were on Ernie's heels laughing and shouting obscenities at Paul.

Paul leapt onto his bike and started it. Tires squealed out of the parking lot as Ernie jumped through the door and brought the shotgun to bear on Paul. Paul ducked, and a loud boom chased him from the lot. He watched in the rearview mirror while Ernie took potshots at him, laughing wildly in the wicked strobe-light illumination of the muzzle flashes that grew smaller and smaller in Paul's rearview as he raced out of Armbister and into the vast desert of the Texas night.

7

Paul sat up on the couch, arms folded over his stomach not because it hurt but mostly to reassure himself that he still had a body, that he was no longer drifting in the darkness. His consciousness had tethered itself to a body that felt like his own. And he knew the Stranger was nearby, watching him. "How long was I out?"

"Enough time for them to decide you're guilty," came the reply. The Stranger's voice had a softness that comforted Paul, making him feel safe. The wind still blew outside, though not as hard as before, and it carried a soothing quality that reminded Paul of the Stranger's voice.

"How long?"

"Since last night, and I wouldn't go around saying your name is Paul Reynolds. You're kinda famous, man."

"Jesus."

The Stranger laughed. "Not that kind of famous." His soft laughter resonated in the small room that formed the cage walls of Paul's blackness. It sounded pleasant and not in any way mean-spirited. Just the same, it irritated Paul. How could a person laugh at this? "One for the books, man, in the middle of the desert and you crash into a fuckin' boat," the Stranger said when his laughter settled enough for him to speak.

"Stop laughing," Paul said, facing the direction of the Stranger's voice. The Stranger stopped, but Paul knew he still must have been smiling. He imagined a disembodied smile floating in the darkness, faceless, like a crazy Cheshire cat. "A boat?" Paul finally asked, curiosity piqued.

The Stranger chuckled one last time. "I was out walkiendo, you know, like I always do. Anyways, I'm getting my morning exercise, I hear they say it's good for the heart, anyway, I'm walking along, and I come across some clothes that had blown out of a torn up old backpack, so I follow this trail of clothes, and it leads to you. You're lyin' there all bloody and beat up and twisted, and there's a big crack on the visor of your helmet so I figure you're muerto, right. Anyways, no sense in lettin' your stuff go to waste, so I start in to goin' through your pack. Sorry, I'm poor, and besides I thought you were dead." The Stranger barked a half laugh.

"So Mercury—that's my dog that's with me, she's sniffin' your face and you twitch. She's actually part coyote —kind of a half-breed like me. So anyway, man, I feel your pulse and sure as shit you're alive. Never mind your bike is wrapped up around that old ski boat someone abandoned out on the highway last month and you're lyin' near two hundred feet from where your bike hit that boat, swear to God—a damn boat." He laughed again, sounding like he might cry from the laughter.

"Sorry," he said, the laughter fading, a gentle breeze disappearing. "So I look at your wallet and yes sir your name's Paul Reynolds. The guy from the radio, fallen out of my own little piece of sky just like that, so I says to Mercury and she barks and I know she's sayin' I gotta take you in. That I can't just leave you for los cops because they're gonna be lookin' for you.

"So, I stuff what I can into your pack and drag you back here. You've been out hard since last night, and I've been lookin' at your stuff. I liked the notebook with all the UFO pictures in it. That was real interesting," the Stranger said. "I didn't ever know anybody who followed that stuff in them magazines like you, but I found it real interesting. I never seen a UFO myself, but I know a guy says he's seen one. Lots of people do. I ain't sayin' they don't."

Paul listened to the voice drift out of the darkness. "There aren't any UFOs, it's just—never mind. Who are you?"

"My name is Sergio."

Paul nodded, assuming the Stranger—Sergio—could see the gesture. No reason to assume not. "Am I going to be all right? I mean my eyes?"

"They look fine. I was a medic in the Army once, so I can say you will be okay."

Paul considered this for a moment. He had a million questions to ask the voice in the darkness that had named itself Sergio. He wanted his things. He wanted out. He wanted to remember. The past had become diffused and incoherent. His life seemed like reception from another state—another planet—fuzzy and distorted with no patterns, no logic. He didn't speak the language, but he understood the intonations. "I didn't kill anybody," he said. He couldn't make any other words come out, and anyways it seemed best to settle the big issue first.

"Radio says you were all talkin' about having that guy's head in your pack." Sergio let this hang. Did he sound impressed?

Paul's memory drifted back to hazy words at Ed's. Ernie's, he corrected himself. That was it: Ernie's with the flickering 'T.' Flickering like the blue spark.

"I didn't find it, though," Sergio added in a weird show of understanding.

"Am I safe here?"

"Safe as me," Sergio replied slowly. Choosing his words carefully, Paul noticed. "You hungry?" Sergio asked in a new, hurried kind of way.

Paul's stomach tightened at the thought of eating. Anything. "Yeah," he said with relief.

A moment passed, and Paul listened to a wooden chair creak as it gave up Sergio's weight. The chair amplified Sergio's heft, and Paul pictured him as a stout man. Probably with an overhanging gut considering the way he seemed to put away the beer.

Sergio's soft footsteps receded a short distance. Where they stopped, a wooden cabinet swooshed open. Sergio removed things from the cabinet, creating dull thudding sounds that bounced from the counter where the unseen objects were placed. Paul tried to form images, but while the sounds seemed distinct and firm as stone, he couldn't quite turn them into concrete images in his mind. His mental movie lacked focus and gave only an incomplete version of the world. Clattering metal, a sort of cacophonous high-pitched noise, followed the sound of a drawer sliding open. A silverware drawer, Paul guessed.

Paul imagined Sergio fishing for a fork or a knife, and he felt relieved that the man at least owned silverware. Shifting metal and then silence indicated that Sergio had found whatever he sought. A sudden vacuum pop made Paul think of peanut butter, and as he thought it, the distinct smell reached his nostrils. Did he smell it, he wondered, because he invented the correct interpretation for the sounds, or was the smell real? Nevertheless, his brain screamed: Peanut Butter! "Peanut Butter?" he asked aloud.

Sergio stopped rustling, and now Paul could discern Sergio's breath. Sergio's voice drifted through the dark. "Can you see?"

"I smelled it."

Sergio gave a halfhearted grunt, made a few more kitchen type noises, then walked back to Paul's corner of the dark. "Put your hand out."

Paul extended his arm in the direction that felt most like front. As if by magic, accompanied by the sounds of Sergio sitting back in the rickety chair, a soft mass materialized in Paul's outstretched hand. He closed his fingers slightly, testing the spring of the bread. It felt fresh. Paul lifted the sandwich towards the center of his consciousness because he knew his mouth would be just below it.

The bread tasted old, but still soft, still a long way from stale. The peanut butter dried his mouth, sucked the moisture from every saliva gland, and made him feel as if the whole desert were inside him. He forced the gooey texture down his throat, his body screaming for a drink.

"Need a beer?"

For a moment, Paul wondered if Sergio might be clairvoyant, but he quickly understood that Sergio could see him and the fleeting grimace that must have crossed his face. Paul jotted a mental note: *Just because I can't see him doesn't mean he can't see me.* It seemed important to remember, a thing he would always have to bear in mind.

"Yeah." And as Paul said the word, a warm bottle materialized from the nothing to fill his hand. He took a sip. Lager. Major American type macrobrew. He didn't care that it was warm. He smiled. "Warm beer? No jelly?"

"No electricity."

Paul nodded, anticipating the answer, and bit off a heartier chunk of the PB minus J sandwich. Another sip of the bubbly warm beer. Paul felt his body awaken. Felt the nausea slipping away and lucidity returning, albeit slowly. The food emboldened him. Made him feel more alive. Or at least more sure of the fact that he was alive. Immaterial spirits did not eat. He knew this to be some kind of unavoidable physical or even metaphysical law of being. Ghosts cannot eat. Therefore if he was eating he must be among the living. The blind, but the living. He tore another bite of reassurance from the dry sandwich. When did I start believing in ghosts, he wondered.

"Are you going to take me in and collect your reward money?" Paul realized this might not be such a bad idea almost as he spoke it. It seemed more certain than staying here. He could ditch the weed, if he even still had it, get to a hospital and blame his not coming forward on a fear of Ernie's shotgun followed by the crash. He would claim he was lucky to be alive, and would one of you good doctors please fix my eyes? Paul waited a second or two before adding as extra incentive: "You could get your electricity turned back on."

Sergio laughed politely. "I ain't even hooked up," he responded with a smile in his voice.

"What about money, though? Everyone needs money," Paul said through his last bite of dusty peanut butter sandwich.

"No way." Sergio's voice sounded blacker than Paul had heard it before. Paul imagined that if he could see Sergio's face, it would have clouded over. Paul tried not to think of reasons why Sergio would want to keep him around. *Why should he be so emphatic about me not leaving?*

Paul swallowed the last bit of sandwich. He rubbed the tops of his bare legs. For a moment he worried he was naked, until his palm brushed the hem of his boxers. He felt his body, nearby in the darkness, unseen.

Sergio's chair creaked, and he began to pace around the muted room. Metal slid on wood then went suddenly quiet as Paul imagined Sergio picking up a large metal object that must have been lying on top of a wooden table.

Paul's skin grew damp as he imagined all the large metal objects that might be put to dark purposes. Sweat condensed on his forehead, neck, and armpits. He felt danger, could almost smell it like they say dogs can. He knew without understanding that something was wrong. Some unknown and inscrutable convention had been violated, and suddenly Sergio felt more like a stranger than the familiar peanut butter and beer bearing voice of concern from a few moments earlier, the voice that had rescued him.

Paul felt around the couch. His hands probed the edges, racing along the rim of the cushion and in quick reconnaissance gestures into the empty space beyond the couch. Paul tried to make sense of the world Out There.

Paul's palm brushed against a wooden surface at about knee level. The surface of this other, wooden, world was a foot from the edge of the couch. He placed his other hand on it, and together they felt the flat, scratched surface. Paul's hands saw a coffee table.

Sergio's maddeningly pleasant chuckle drifted over to Paul. It sounded as if it came from ten feet away. Directly in front of him. Paul sat straight up and pointed his head in the direction of the laugh. It grew louder and more defined as he did so, but Paul understood it to be a trick of his shift in perspective and not in Sergio's volume.

"I ain't gonna run you in," Sergio said.

Before Paul could summon a response, a door opened. The wind grew louder, and Paul guessed this to be the outside door. Directly in front of him. Probably eight feet beyond the coffee table. If he could see, he thought, he would be staring straight at the door. With this, his world grew. He felt there could be a way out, even though he had no clue what might lie beyond that beckoning door. The universe expanded rapidly, the horizons falling back farther and farther with each hour of wakefulness. The world beyond himself. The world beyond the Stranger. The world beyond that door. Was it day or night? The darkness in no way changed when the door opened, so maybe darkness held the desert as firmly as it held Paul. The door slammed shut, and Sergio was gone.

Paul wanted to follow him, desperate to ask more questions. He pushed himself up off the couch, soaring through the darkness. He forgot the beer between his thighs until it poured out of the bottle onto and down his bare legs. Instinctively, Paul shifted his legs, and the bottle fell to the ground with a low thump. Where the hell are my clothes, he wondered. He felt most at Sergio's mercy because he wore only his underwear.

Paul ventured a hasty step forward, towards the door, forgetful of the table until his knee connected with the wood. Hard. Paul yelped and stumbled sideways, impacting with a sharp wooden corner on his way to the ground. By the time the ground finally met him, he had fallen through space for days. His knee throbbed like jelly, and his shoulder burned where the table had removed a chunk of it. Lying on the ground, feeling the warm blood on his shoulder and the sticky beer on his legs, Paul realized his instincts were correct: This was indeed a coffee table.

He tried to take comfort in the fact that Sergio hadn't witnessed his first adventure away from the couch and his subsequent defeat by the coffee table. He imagined the soft, friendly laughter that would have followed his fall.

Paul lay crumpled by the table, not moving except to breathe. The impossibility and sheer weight—beyond weight, pure gravity—of his situation settled over him. He wondered if he had been sucked into a black hole and then decided it was more like being a dolphin stuck in a tuna net. Wrong place. Wrong time. He felt queasy for liking tuna sandwiches so much as his hands began to make sense of the surface on which he was lying.

One hand moved over the rough ground. The floor felt as if Sergio had never swept it. Only when he began to dig a bit with his aching fingers did Paul realize he was lying on a dirt floor. He felt around to make sure he wasn't just lying on a hole in the floor. One hand found the leg of the hated coffee table. Then felt dirt as far as his hands could feel.

No electricity. No floor. No other people. Paul's knee began to hurt less, and the throbbing subsided, but still he didn't move. There was no point. Paul thought he might as well be hog-tied and blindfolded. Might as well be dead. A shiver crept down his spine and caused his whole body to tremble for a moment when he thought that he might soon be. The ground felt cold, and the beer on his legs grew chilly. His fingers brushed the thick quicksand-like mud puddle on the 'floor' in front of the couch where the beer spilled. The sickening odor of spilled beer drifted to his nostrils.

Paul wondered in a state of detached and hopeless paranoia if Sergio ate people or tortured them or raped them. Maybe he was some kind of crazy separatist mail-bomber or a religious nut living the penitent life of some obscure and half-understood personal faith. The blue spark tore through the flimsy rags of Paul's consciousness, re-igniting the almost forgotten headache as it went.

8

Soft light appears, ghostly as from a full moon, but there is no moon in the sky. The motorcycle rumbles through the preternaturally bright night of the broken landscape. Rocks, cacti, and millions of stars wheel by outside my visor. The helmet and the speed, amplified by the beam of the glowing headlamp, cut peripheral vision down to just a few feet on either side of the road. I feel as if I am racing through a tunnel. As if my destination is predetermined and there is only one direction I can go. There is no light at the end of this tunnel.

The speedometer needle bobs steadily at a hundred miles-per-hour.

A pair of halogen-bright lights swoop down from the sky and blink on and off behind me. Their reflection in the rearview mirror catches my attention.

An eerie wailing fills the air, cross-fading and drowning out the thunder of the bike. It is louder than my engine.

A huge white light dominates the road behind me. Blue lights twinkle above it, and menacing yellow lights glow beneath. Together they obliterate the dim glow of the stars.

I twist the throttle and separate from the lights in a burst of speed. They accelerate perfectly in time with me, and I admire the precision with which the lights stay together and keep pace with me.

The lights pursue me over the blacktop. I try to watch the road and watch the lights mostly with my mirrors, but occasionally I can steal a glance over my shoulder. I find it increasingly difficult to watch the road ahead. I am mesmerized by that which cannot be.

The lights go out. The whistling sound stops. Relief washes over me. I find myself alone in the not-quite-dark dream light, and the sudden roar of the engine that replaces the soothing whistle jars me into watching the road, which I think I had forgotten was there. I swerve away from an old tire discarded by some rig.

I glance back over my shoulder to see if the lights will stay gone.

They blaze back to existence all at once. Closer than ever. The whistling is now a jet engine roar.

The road curves away. The tires leave the asphalt. An old ski boat, abandoned on the side of the road, races towards me. In black letters, the words Anne's Vacation *name the boat. The bike bounces over the broken ground at nearly a hundred miles an hour.*

   Straight towards the boat.

9

Paul lay on the floor for what seemed to be hours. He drifted through the darkness searching for seams, an astronaut lost and untethered on a doomed space walk far from any sun. He felt his space ship drift farther away, the crew forgetting him and him knowing that not only would help never come, it never could. Earthly sounds, harsh and breaking, emanated through the walls from outside. Metal on wood. The sounds developed order and a soothing rhythm. Paul remembered a dream, but as he woke it evaporated under the heat of his lucidity until he only remembered it had something to do with the crash.

Eventually, he decided to climb back up onto the couch. He grasped the hard edge of the coffee table and levered himself up to his knees. The knee that had hit the table quavered when he pressed on it with his weight. It felt bruised. Paul slid onto the couch and leaned back into it. As he settled into a comfortable position, Sergio opened the door and clomped back into the small room.

Paul listened to Sergio stride past him and into the kitchen area. He clattered the silverware drawer and opened a cabinet. A pop and Paul could smell peanut butter again. Another pop—this time a can—indicated something to drink. Sergio walked towards the place where Paul believed himself to be and placed some items on the coffee table. The chair accepted Sergio's weight with a wooden groan.

Paul leaned forward and let his hands explore the surface of the table. He discovered a warm can, a sandwich, and a banana. The banana excited Paul the most, and he picked it up and peeled it. He bit the end off the banana, savoring its sweet taste. He picked up the can. Expecting soda, he took a large sip and tasted beer. The warm lager in no way complemented the banana, and he grimaced at the taste-sensation of the beer foam that rose in his mouth as the beer slid over the sugar on his teeth. Paul wished Sergio had water. Legends claimed astronauts got cyanide tablets in case they got lost. Paul guessed Sergio and he were taking a slower approach: beer.

"I'm out of bottled water. Sorry. Never thought warm beer would be good did you, though?" Again, Sergio seemed to read Paul's mind. Probably he was just reading his face. Weird, Paul thought, how the mind when disoriented by the loss of its main sensor can forget all the external realities so very quickly. He hoped he would start remembering and thereby reduce Sergio's apparent clairvoyance.

Paul took a slow sip from his beer and nodded. He nodded mostly to force himself to relate, or at least appear to be relating, to the tenth dimension external world purporting to lie outside his darkness as if in another universe. Paul found the real world increasingly difficult to believe in, as if vision were nothing more than a wormhole between the brain and the outside. He imagined himself falling into his own black hole, stretched out like a spaghetti strand, his screams lost in the gravity well.

"Where were you going?" Sergio asked. A signal from the outside pulling Paul back into shape if not into light.

Paul thought of evasions. No point. He tried to project certainty through the void, but in fact he had lost his sense of what emotions, tics, and gestures would play across his body as he spoke. He held wooden still. "East coast. Appalachian Trail, maybe."

"Why?"

"I don't know. Anywhere. I didn't have a destination. I just wanted to go. Shoot some film. Smoke some dope. Get away from the deserts and the west."

"It's gone."

"What? The camera?"

"The west." Sergio said. "And the dope, and the camera, I guess. I didn't see it."

"You didn't see the camera?"

"No."

"But it was in my pack. You said you got my pack."

"Lo siento, man."

"You left it? Jesus. That was all I had."

"You're free to go anytime you like."

"And where would I go?"

Paul was met for a brief moment with Sergio's good-natured laugh. It was the laugh of a large yet gentle man. The situation made the laugh seem more ominous—fatal—than it probably was. "To Hell, I imagine," Sergio said. He stopped laughing, then added, "or you could go look for your pot. Except you can't see. I guess you're done for."

Paul wondered how old Sergio was. "Why aren't you turning me in?"

"You did not kill him." All-knowing. Matter-of-fact. Certain beyond even Paul's recollections.

"How do you know? Hell, maybe I did and I just don't remember. Maybe my circuits are all so cross-wired I don't remember anything, or maybe I'm just dreaming up a way out so I can believe I didn't do it when I face one of those polygraph things. How can you be so sure it wasn't me? I'm not."

"What do you *believe*?"

The question, the odd phrasing, and Sergio's emphasis on 'believe' caught Paul off-guard. He wondered if he had always paid such close attention to intonation and inflection before now or if his ears were learning to see the gestures in words. "What do I believe?" he repeated.

"About what happened. How you wound up here. You should be up around Tennessee by now. Maybe."

"I must have crashed into that boat. I'm wanted."

Sergio laughed, his voice like bubbles rising from a whirlpool. "You got shipwrecked," he said.

"It's not funny. None of this is funny."

"Oh, it is. Muy funny."

"I crashed my bike!"

"Why did you crash?" Sergio asked, jump cutting to a weird German accent like a cartoon shrink. The accent was dead-on perfect.

"Because—" Paul started.

In his head, Paul saw himself on a motorcycle careening into a large sailboat in broad daylight. The image played out as a cartoon. *Why did I crash?* "I wasn't tired. I didn't fall asleep. That jerk was shooting at me just before it happened. At least that's how I remember it. Maybe... Was I shot?"

"I saw no wounds. No gunshot wounds."

Paul nodded. Again, that empty gesture for inhabitants of the foreign world beyond the velvet ink darkness.

"How does this happen? I can't see."

A sip of beer, taken in contemplation, rippled in tiny echoes through the dark. Paul waited for some kind of knowledgeable answer.

"I gotta fix my truck. Want to come watch? I mean listen," Sergio corrected himself abruptly. As if politely trying not to remind Paul of the one fact he couldn't escape. The one thing he actually did know with certainty.

"Why don't you have electricity, Sergio?"

"I'm poor."

"You have a truck and you're fixing it so you can afford gas," Paul said. Thinking about a truck made Paul feel better. Safer. With a truck there was a way out. Not that he could drive, but at least he might not have to walk.

An empty can crush exploded nearby, and the reduced can landed firmly on the wooden table. "I don't have electricity because I don't want to be seen."

"Where do you get gas and beer?"

"I don't want to be seen, you know, officially." Sergio paused. "I sell things. Statues that I carve, mainly."

Paul thought of the heavy metal object rising from the wood, the knocking sounds outside the door. An image formed out of the sounds in his mind. "You use an ax."

"Yes."

"Was it on a table? Over there?" Paul lifted his arm, extending a finger in the direction he remembered the sounds coming from. He waited for a reply.

Sergio laughed. "A little to the left, but not bad."

Paul adjusted the direction of his pointing hand, moving it slightly to the left. "There?"

"Sí. Yes. It's a hatchet. Over on a table. Not five feet from where your finger points."

Paul smiled and then bit his dry lower lip. He let out an exhaling laugh, surprised at his guesswork and feeling slightly more sure of himself.

"You listen well," Sergio complimented. "They say the blind can see with their ears."

"I want to see with my eyes."

"Sí. Sí."

Sergio shifted in his chair.

Paul took the last sip of his beer and found himself surprised to actually enjoy the warm, frothy brew. A belch rose up and out of his mouth.

"Getting towards the end of the beer."

"Are you some kind of religious monk?"

"I stay quiet. Invisible."

"Invisible," Paul repeated.

"It seems to be working," Sergio laughed. "I have my first guest in nearly thirty years, and you can't see me. But you drink all my beer, so now I have to go get more, which means I have to sell some statues, which means I have to get my truck fixed up sooner."

Sergio stood up.

Paul listened to his bulky movements, heard his hands grasp the aluminum cans, slightly crushing them as they left the table with a quick wooden knock. Sergio took two steps, and then as far as Paul could sense, Sergio disappeared into the sonic darkness, replaced by the sound of the shifting wind outside the room. He moved his head from side to side, straining to hear some sign of Sergio's presence, but he had vanished into black air.

From another, soundless, part of the room, Paul heard a sharp intake of breath followed by another that then settled into Sergio's normal breathing. Paul turned his face towards the sound of the breath, which was on the opposite side of the darkness from where Sergio's sounds had disappeared when he held his breath.

"I'm pretty quiet when I want to be, but you found me anyway." Sergio's voice sounded pleased, almost fatherly. "I was watching you listen to me. You always seem to know where I am so I figured I'd check how well you can find me."

"You just disappeared from my... perception."

"If I could do that to someone whose eyes worked, I would be like a crazy Houdini."

After a few moments of silence, Sergio took another few steps and set the cans down, along with whatever else he was holding.

"I'm tired of sitting here," Paul said. "I'd like to get up and move my legs a bit."

Sergio shuffled towards Paul. He clamped a firm hand down on Paul's shoulder. "You'll be okay. I'm going to show you around my home. So you don't have to bump into everything. Then we'll go outside."

Sergio took Paul's hand in his. His rough skin told Paul the man had worked hard at doing whatever he did. Paul noticed wrinkles and calluses on the large solid hand. He imagined Sergio to be a firm handshaker. "Where do you live?"

"In the desert. This guy over in Austin owns the land. Some environmental preservation dude. No hunting, no cattle, no farming, no drilling. I'm alone out here since no one has any business being here. I guess you'd call me a squatter. That's why I don't got no power or water." Sergio laughed. "Hell, I ain't even got no floor."

Sergio gave Paul's arm a gentle tug, and Paul felt himself rise off the couch. Sergio did most of the lifting, and for the first time since awakening, Paul stood on his own two feet. His knees wobbled. His leg muscles twitched from not being used since he'd fled Ernie's, but they soon settled down and supported his weight.

Sergio put Paul's arm through his own and helped him shuffle sideways to avoid walking into the coffee table again. Paul let Sergio guide him around the treacherous black room.

"There's only three rooms here," Sergio began, "My room, the kitchen, and the main room. Really, it's all one room, but I have some old curtains separating them. Built the place myself. Wanted to have me some walls, but I just never got around to it," Sergio laughed at this. "Anyways lucky for you."

"How so?"

"With curtains you can't bang yourself up so bad when you walk into them."

Paul let Sergio guide him through the house. He listened to Sergio's friendly voice explain where each cabinet, each table, each chair stood while counting off the steps between large items and the door. One from couch to coffee table. Eight from coffee table to door. Slide left, back one, turn and two more to the 'kitchen' that consisted of a table, a shelf, a cabinet and a large cooler to keep the bugs out and not so much the cold in, Sergio explained.

Objects and shapes formed in Paul's imagination. Everything second hand and made of old wood. Paul touched a shelf near the door. It held some books and the wood was worn smooth. His mind became a sonar map of the room. A map built on sound and touch. As the vocabulary of sounds grew, the darkness filled with mass and a sort of homey topography. Paul felt like a submarine, blind beneath the waves, navigating through invisible canyons and valleys by the sonar sound of Sergio's voice. It wasn't melodic like a dolphin's or mechanical like a submarine's ping-ping but warm and committed to seeing that Paul didn't have any further run-ins with the furniture.

"Basically," Sergio explained, "front door is eight steps from the coffee table. With your back to the front door my bedroom is left and the kitchen area is right."

"It's going to take a while to get it."

"You will. People do what they have to."

"You built this place yourself?"

"Sí," Sergio shuffled away from Paul, slightly. "Many years ago. I made it from adobe. Some wood. Things I find around."

"Like one of those pueblos?"

"Yeah, like one of them."

"Are you Indian?"

"Umm… well, my family was Mexican… I fought in the US Army. So I guess you could say my blood is red."

"You sound kind of Mexican."

"I guess I sort of look it too, but most Mexicans are at least part Indian with European. No difference really, except language. I forgot most of the Spanish I knew. Never knew no Indian languages."

"Why did you settle here?"

"Why were you going east?"

Paul opened his mouth to answer, but he thought of Sergio's sudden evasiveness as the questions became more personal, and he thought better and closed it again. He shrugged.

"Me too," came the response to the invisible shrug. "Let's go outside."

The front door creak-creaked open and fell back behind Paul with a snap. Sergio stepped away from Paul as soon as they were outside. Paul hoped that the darkness would lighten a bit or redden when he got outside under the blazing sun, but the darkness stayed black as before. He felt the sun burn on his face, his bare arms and legs. It almost felt good. He could smell the wind as it drifted over him, a gentle but still hot breeze. The wind carried messages; images flashed in his mind: crude oil, decaying plants, some flowers, a nearby animal, the sharp odor of gasoline—faint but noticeable. "It's evening," Paul ventured.

"It's about five."

"It's warmer out here, but cooler than at midday. I can feel it. Almost smell it. Like the day is too old to carry on."

Paul stood under the desert sun and imagined it must still be a good forty-five degrees above the horizon. He figured he'd use a two-fifty on the shutter and an f/22 for maximum depth of field if he were to photograph Sergio standing nearby. He tried not to think about his lack of sight. He smelled gasoline nearby. He heard fast, quiet footsteps approach, crunching invisible over the earth.

The footsteps stopped as suddenly as they started and Paul froze. The steps did not come from human feet.

"Venga aquí," Sergio whispered, and Paul realized with some relief that Sergio had spoken to a dog.

"Who is that?"

"Mercury." The footsteps resumed and padded over to the part of the darkness from which Sergio's voice emanated. Sergio and Mercury stood to the left of Paul, which Paul noted in the back of his mind would have to be south since he generally faced the sun. Paul turned towards Sergio's voice.

"She's an old half-breed. Coyote and dog mix-up. I give her some food, but she doesn't like peanut butter. It sticks to the roof of her mouth."

An image appeared in Paul's mind, playing across his mental projection screen: Paul offering a family dog some peanut butter in distant childhood. It spends the next few minutes licking maniacally, almost painfully, to get the gooey substance off the roof of its mouth. A ghost smile from childhood crept across his adult lips, the picture rendered more absurd when imagining Sergio, grown and in the desert getting the same laughs from a coyote.

"You know what I mean, then."

For a moment Paul didn't, but then he remembered Sergio, living in a world of light, could see the invisible smile on his face. Paul made a mental note to stop broadcasting every thought, every emotion to any one in the world with a pair of eyes to see. He didn't think he gave this much away before the accident. Or he thought he didn't. Maybe he was just becoming more aware of it. He felt vulnerable because he couldn't read Sergio so well. Maybe that was it: Sergio remained capable of hiding so much more.

Paul's smile disappeared as he tried to school his features. He decided to pay closer attention to his reactions, his emotions and gestures. He could feel himself smile and nod and shudder, but he had no sense of Sergio's true state. Were his eyes laughing when he laughed or was he staring hatefully through Paul? Mentally sharpening that ax blade or tying a noose.

Something dry and furry brushed against Paul's fingers, hovering over his hand. Paul allowed the animal to sniff him before he touched its snout. Paul followed the dog's coarse fur to its face and scratched it behind its small leathery ears. "Part coyote, huh. Dangerous?"

"You should hear her howl." Sergio's voice became soft and faraway.

"Her? Isn't her name Mercury?"

"Yes."

"Mercury was a god, not a goddess."

"It's just a name I liked."

"What color is she?" Paul asked.

"She'll tell you. If you listen."

"Excuse me?"

"Just ask. Listen close. She'll tell."

Paul shook his head. You've been out here a very long time, haven't you, Sergio, a long, long, long time, Paul thought, the weirdo buzzers blaring inside his brain. "I didn't know animals did talk," Paul finally managed. He hoped for a response. A justification.

The wind gusted through nearby plants. Mercury's nose touched Paul's dangling hand. "Yellowish brown?" Paul finally guessed, making his assumption based on memories of pictures of coyotes in books and on National Geographic specials. It worried him that he couldn't imagine yellow as perfectly as he once thought he could. He remembered hearing that men did not—could not—dream in color even though they thought they did. *Maybe we can't remember colors either.* "She's yellow."

"See? She told you. Good girl."

"I guessed," Paul responded, sure he was deflating Sergio a bit and feeling sorry about that. He felt bad about shooting down the beliefs of the man who was helping him. Old habits died hard. "How long have you had her?"

"As long as I can even remember," Sergio said quietly. "I don't know for sure. Seems like she's been here forever, though."

Paul knelt down to pet Mercury a bit more. Talking animals aside, Paul always loved dogs. He tried to imagine the yellow color of the coarse fur he stroked, but all he saw was a garish primary version of it like a child's crayon drawing of a yellow dog despite knowing she would be a sandy, dirty shade of yellow.

As he thought about color he began to wonder whether he would see the blue spark again or if that was simply a side effect of stumbling back to the reality of Sergio's couch. He hoped he would see it again, or remember it or however he had sensed it. In point of fact, he did not know.

Paul remembered an argument he once had in high school with a friend. Paul had said with all the conviction he could muster that only black and white photography could be considered art. The friend denied this, but Paul insisted all his life and still refused to shoot in color. If there were some kind of karmic law this would surely count as payback, Paul thought. Instead it was devastating. Paul could already feel himself beginning to yearn for color; he realized he would very soon only remember the world in black and white, and after that the white would drain away and he would remember and know only black. He felt his world shriveling into an extinct universe with no starlight and nothing left but radio sources to guide him through what was left of the burned-out sky.

10

When night fell, the temperature cooled slightly, not a major temperature drop but enough to provide welcome relief from the heat and for Paul to be able to distinguish day from night. Paul and Sergio enjoyed the warmth of a crackling fire and sipped warm beer from the thin cans. Twigs snapped and broke in the fire like ladyfingers while the ever-present desert wind never seemed to still. The far-off calls of animals wandering through the night occasionally rose above the fire.

Paul tried to ignore the sound of a rattlesnake that seemed a bit too close. He listened to the hissing rattle and wondered if it was in striking distance but relaxed upon realizing that Sergio would have been worried too—unless snakes talked and were harmless. Maybe his hearing was getting better. Maybe the snake was far and Sergio couldn't hear it.

Sergio crushed his can, its sound momentarily echoing through Paul's darkness. It preceded an impact sound, much crackling and hissing, as Sergio tossed the sound into the fire.

"I can hear so much. More than I used to. It's so quiet out here," Paul said.

"A person's eyes make a lot of noise."

"That sounds very wise, Sergio. Are you going all New Age Indian on me?"

Sergio popped open another beer and took a long sloppy gulp. He swallowed then belched. Paul could smell the beer on his stale breath.

"I like to sleep out here," Sergio responded. He ignored Paul's slight.

Paul took another sip of the beer and scooted himself closer to the protection of the fire. The change in sounds and temperature had signaled beyond doubt that night had come and with it a growing uneasiness, a sense of supreme isolation and vulnerability. Paul wished they were indoors but grew angry with himself for being afraid. Previous to losing his sight, Paul cherished quiet nights by the campfire. Now he just felt like an easy target.

He listened for the rattlesnake, but the night did not give up its sounds just for wishes, and Paul imagined it had found a rat or some desert frog to gorge itself on so it could leave him alone. On the sonic horizon, the eerie sound of a coyote drifted to Paul's ears. It was followed by another and another until a whole pack seemed to be singing in the vast darkness.

"Tell me about your notebook," Sergio asked, his voice soft and completely at home as if he were just another of the harsh and wild denizens of the desert quietly going about his inscrutable business.

"My notebook?"

Sergio sipped his beer. Stifled a belch. "With all those pictures of the flying saucers. Can't you tell they're fake? Those pictures are terrible."

Paul sipped his beer. He was reaching the bottom of the can, and the beer was starting to taste flat and stale. "I took those pictures," Paul said, his voice betraying not a little pride. "All of them, so, yeah, I know they're fake."

"Why?"

"It's my job," Paul said.

"Your job?"

"I make fake UFO photos and sell them."

Sergio laughed. "People buy these?"

"Sure, magazines do—tabloids, you know—it's proof we're not alone. Seeing is believing."

"How do you make the spacecraft?"

"Didn't you find the Frisbee in my pack?"

"The Frisbee is the UFO?"

"Yeah."

"I couldn't tell."

"Thank you," Paul said.

"That ain't no compliment, man. It's disgusting, you know, to prey on people's beliefs. Their fantasies."

"Sergio, it's just entertainment."

"Surely not for many."

Paul found himself laughing at the seriousness with which Sergio seemed to be taking this. He felt good, buzzed by the beer, outdoors enjoying the fire. He almost began to forget he was blind. Maybe his eyes were just closed and he could open them at any time.

"What? Why are you so happy all of a sudden. I don't know if I like you so much right now."

"I'm sorry," Paul managed. He stopped laughing. "I'm just a bit buzzed, I guess. Sorry."

"It was busted anyway."

"Sergio, you don't actually believe in UFOs do you?"

"People see things. I don't know what."

Paul let out another short laugh. "Trust me, Sergio, there's no such thing. I'd be out of work if there was." Paul finished his beer. He crushed the can and tossed it aside. He listened to it bounce across the ground. "Can I have another one?"

Sergio popped another beer and placed it in Paul's waiting hand. "That's your last one. I'm running low. We gotta get the truck fixed tomorrow. Go get some more supplies."

Paul sipped the beer. It tasted better each time he had one of the warm bland brews. Maybe there were beer goggles for the taste buds, Paul mused, as he sipped and enjoyed the beer.

"You're out of work anyway," Sergio began continuing the conversation from earlier, bouncing from one thought train to another.

Paul had almost forgotten the previous talk as he savored his last round of mediocre beer.

"Even if you get to see again," Sergio continued, "I don't know where your camera is."

"It wasn't even on my bike?"

"I didn't check your bike."

Paul slumped forward a bit. Even though his cameras were of no use to him, at least in the short term he reminded himself optimistically, he still wanted them. They were his... friends almost. His companions. "Those cameras were all I had that mattered. Without them, I'm screwed."

"The cops probably have your cameras."

Paul imagined the police swarming over his motorcycle, taking his beloved cameras and tagging them away as evidence or to be sold at some police auction. He worried about the film that was in one of the bodies. Exposed film. Some pretty good shots he'd gotten back in Arizona. Back when he could see. He wanted to scream. He wanted to jump up and shake Sergio and ask why he hadn't saved the cameras, the only things that mattered.

The snake rattled again, and Paul fixed his thoughts back on the snake, which sounded farther away now. It was retreating. Going to look for more food. Paul thought about the snake finding him before Sergio had. Or a mountain lion. Or a buzzard. He shuddered at the thought of lying blind and lost in the desert being eaten by wild animals. Waking on Sergio's couch had been a lot more beneficial to his sanity than waking in the desert would have been. Or in a cell. And here was this lone man whose medical training somehow obligated him to take care of Paul, himself a stranger in Sergio's universe. Paul felt bad about ridiculing Sergio. Crazy the man may be, but he had saved his life.

"Why were you a medic, Sergio?"

Sergio laughed a soft laugh. A sip of beer punctuated the laugh, and Paul took another swallow of his as well.

"I was living in America, and I was a citizen and so had to pay the price of being a citizen," Sergio remembered. "I was drafted to go fight in Vietnam. I thought it was wrong to kill." He laughed again. This time the laugh sounded self-deprecatory and ironic. "I was young and stupid."

"Now you don't?"

"Now I don't."

"I see."

This made Sergio laugh, and Paul joined him.

All Sergio could manage was a chuckling, "Do you?"

Sergio stopped laughing. "I never should have been a medic," Sergio said.

"Why?"

"When I was little... I always wanted to be a pirate. I imagined I would sail the oceans, live on some little island in the South Pacific or the Caribbean. I would be my own man, and do as I pleased. I would raise hell, and people would shit in their pants when they saw my boat coming at them. It would be the end of the road, amigo." He grunted and took a noisy sip of his beer and then another one. Paul heard each sip, each gurgle of beer leaving the can and each swallow. One's eyes do make a lot of noise. He was beginning to see with his ears. Sergio's face was troubled with age and sorrow. Paul knew it; he could hear it

"We're violent apes, Paul. Violent apes."

11

Paul woke on the couch and spent a few minutes stretching muscles and listening to metal bang on metal. The sounds came from outside the small house, the walls muffling the noise and taking the sharp edge off. Paul recognized the familiar sounds: wrenches on engine. His stomach tightened and rumbled slightly as he swung his feet over the edge of the couch and sat up.

Wishing he could see even a small change in the darkness, just enough lightening to discern day from night, he stood and stepped around the coffee table and carefully maneuvered across the room. He stepped on a pair of shoes and stooped to try them on. They fit his feet perfectly, and Paul felt lucky to have stumbled over his own shoes on the way to the door. He inched over the eight long steps between coffee table and door, feeling the air with his outstretched arms as he traversed the room. He arrived at the door without hitting anything. He felt proud. Able. He momentarily wished Sergio could be inside to have seen his feat but retracted the silent wish because it made him feel like a child, helpless and dependent on the praise of his savior.

Paul opened the door and stepped into the blaring heat of day, wondering if 'savior' really was the correct term. He had yet to test for sure, to be shown beyond doubt that it wasn't 'captor.' How could he be shown anything, though, when he couldn't see? Hearing must learn to be believing. Touch and taste would be believing or else belief could be a very dark concept for a very long time. Paul wondered how blind people even came to believe in the world at all except as an act of faith.

Sergio's tools clang-clanged, striking and adjusting engine components a short distance from where Paul stood. The smell of gasoline and engine grease mixed with the vague crude smell blowing by on the wind reminded Paul of being in a vast garage. Smelling couldn't be believing, but it was tied into memory because for a moment after walking into the crude air, Paul could almost see himself on his bike, racing into Texas for the first time. He remembered the sights, yet the colors were washed out, fading. How does one describe blue, yellow, red, green? How is light described to one who knows only the darkness of a broken mind?

He lifted his foot and carefully moved it forward. He used the tip of his shoe to feel about for rocks, cacti, holes. He took a tentative step away from the house and towards the sounds and smells of Sergio's truck. He felt untethered as if leaping across a fearsome void from one island of sound to another. With one step, all frame of reference evaporated. The day's early heat drew the sweat from him and quickly soaked the grimy four-day-old t-shirt and boxer shorts that hung wilted and clammy from his body.

Sergio swore, which made Paul realize that he wasn't walking in quite the right direction. He paused and listened. Sergio's breathing labored while unseen hands clumsily worked on the engine. The wind shifted, whisking the gasoline smell away from Paul's nostrils like a curtain brushed hastily aside.

"Sergio," Paul called, not knowing if Sergio even knew he was awake. If he even existed. He could be out here in the desert wind, like a wraith, watching, but not seeing Sergio work.

"Over here. Follow my voice," Sergio said.

Paul turned slightly so that he faced the direction of Sergio's voice. He took careful and deliberate steps through the darkness. Listening to Sergio. Where? Step. Careful. Easy.

"I'll keep talking. I'm just fixing the truck. You can try and start it maybe. I'm almost done." Clank. Bang. "Hang on."

Paul took a step and walked into a fleshy wall.

"Sorry," Sergio said, taking a step and grabbing Paul's upper arm. Paul found himself being escorted off course, around the area where his senses told him the truck stood.

"Know how to drive a standard?" Sergio asked.

"I can't drive."

Sergio pulled the truck's door open with a rusty old groan and pushed Paul into the driver's seat.

"No you can't see," Sergio said, "I bet you can drive, though. They're separate actions. But yeah, I bet you wouldn't get too far."

"Yeah, but—"

"Just start her up, man, when I tell you to. I can't do it all, amigo."

Paul eased himself into the driver's seat. He felt the wheel brush against the tops of his legs. He reached up and grasped the wheel firmly in both hands, ten and two, just like in driver's ed.—the perfect driver—he just had to watch out for boats.

The wheel was thin and made of hard plastic. Not soft and thick like on a newer car. Again Paul marveled at the long years Sergio had been hostage to the desert. He reached for the stick, but his hands didn't connect with it.

He waved his right hand down in front and to the side, searching. He leaned towards the floor.

"Where is it," Paul asked, sitting up and leaning against the bench seat.

"Three on the tree."

"What on the where?"

"Here," Sergio said. He guided Paul's hand to the edge of the steering column. Paul wrapped his hand around the stick that jutted out at nearly forty-five degrees from the wheel.

"I thought you said this was a standard."

"It is. Gear stick is on the wheel."

"I guess it's an older model," Paul mumbled.

Paul moved his feet around beneath the wheel. Clutch, brake, gas. He rested one foot on the clutch and the other near the gas.

He listened to Sergio muck around in the engine.

"Start her up," Sergio yelled from somewhere in front of Paul.

Paul pushed the clutch in, turned the key, and added gas. With a coughing sputter, the engine roared, and the truck lurched forward. Paul took his foot off the gas, and Sergio leapt up beside him. With brute force, Sergio pushed him across the bench and onto the passenger side.

Sergio slammed his door closed and revved the engine a bit, letting it wail like a diving airplane before easing off the gas. As he did, the engine coughed but caught again and then roared steady.

"We're going for a drive," he exclaimed like an excited kid whose parents never allow him to leave the house, his voice filled with relief. The truck lurched forward and began its bumpy off-road trek. "I was worried this time." Sergio's voice darkened as if considering ominous possibilities. "Someday this shit ain't gonna start. I'll be stuck out here."

"Where is here?"

"Too far from anything for an old man. Too far, except from Hell."

Paul nodded, smelling the diesel fumes and wondering how far it was to anywhere besides Hell. "So where are we going then?"

"Town. Armbister. Get some more stuff. Beer, water, food. Got two mouths to feed now."

The truck jerked forward and down over a bump as if pulled on a string by a malevolent bully. The truck careened over another dip, and Paul flew into the air. They landed with a teeth-rattling jolt, and Paul's head whipped back on his neck like the UFO on the end of its string.

"Easy, Sergio."

"Bumpy ride. Sorry. Ain't much I can do, know what I mean?"

More bumps and lurches, and Paul grabbed hold of the armrest on the door with one hand and the bottom of the vinyl bench seat with the other. His fingers ached from clinging to the truck while it bounced over the raw desert. He felt his legs, dirty and sweating, stick to the vinyl seat, and he wished he were wearing his old dead-bug splattered jeans—or anything else—on top of his underwear.

"I don't have any clothes."

"Huh? Oh," Sergio mumbled after probably glancing over and really seeing Paul for the first time that day. Sitting in the same underwear and dirty t-shirt he'd worn the last time he rode into Armbister. "Shit, man. Why didn't you get dressed this morning?"

"You never told me where my backpack was. Or my clothes."

"Oh. I set your pack on that table by the kitchen," Sergio said with a hint of apology threaded through his voice. Then he burst into laughter.

"Stop it," Paul said through truck-rattling clenched teeth. He felt cold despite the heat.

"I'm sorry, it's just—you're in your undies, man." More laughter.

"What if someone sees me? Or we get pulled over or something."

"Then you go to jail. They'll strip you there anyway. What's the big deal?"

"Great."

"Hey, don't worry. They'll probably lock me up too."

Before Paul could follow up, the truck lurched sideways. He clung to the seat to avoid being thrown into Sergio. When the truck firmly returned to the ground, it skidded sideways, a piercing shriek filling the cab. Then the truck hit asphalt, and suddenly the ride smoothed out as Sergio increased the speed. Paul felt the furnace wind pick up and blow in through his window. He rolled the window up to cut the noise. The engine in the old truck rumbled mightily.

"Why would they lock you up?"

"Ahhh," Sergio whispered. "The press begins its interrogation."

"I'm not the press."

"Aiding and abetting," he responded. Sergio added more gas to the engine and clicked on the radio. Tejano music blared out of the trucks tinny, blown speakers.

Paul took the hint. Shut up. Let's not go there. Paul tried not to think of why Sergio might be hiding out, why he was more afraid of the town than Paul. He rolled the window down and let the seething wind blow in his face, bringing him smells from the desert and from the engine.

"Armbister's only about twenty miles down the road. More or less," Sergio yelled over the wind.

"This is such a bad idea."

"What?"

Paul rolled the window up a bit. "This is not good. I don't feel good about this."

"Relax. Nobody notices anything. Besides, I want to keep an eye on you."

"What for?"

"I don't like surprises, that's all."

"Sergio, I'm a wanted man, you remember? I'm kind of a sitting duck." Paul's mind raced. What was this guy up to? Why take chances? Maybe, he's trying to get rid of me, Paul considered.

"Relax."

"Great. I can walk around in my underwear, bang into walls, and stand out to be noticed by anyone with eyes to see."

A great laugh erupted from Sergio. The truck bounced along as its poor shocks put forth a hopeless effort to smooth out the ride. "You paint a great mental picture," Sergio managed to say through his mounting laughter. "But then I guess that's what you do, putting made-up pictures in people's heads."

Paul tried to ignore the laugh. He rolled down the window and felt the convection oven wind pound his ears and whip through his hair.

After a lurching ride with several turns and stops, Sergio cut the engine, and the truck coasted to a smooth stop. The temperature rose the instant the wind died. Paul rolled the window down the rest of the way, but this didn't noticeably improve the air circulation. He could hear traffic whizzing nearby. He could hear the difference between cars and trucks and rigs, and he even heard a low and slow-grumbling engine that must have been a tractor idling down the road. There wasn't a constant flow of traffic. Paul remembered Armbister was too small for that, but he heard every single engine that passed.

"Duck into the floorboard," Sergio ordered.

"Why?"

"Let's just don't take no stupid chances, all right."

Paul eased himself into the floor space in front of his seat. His sweat output doubled, but he was surprised to find that he could fit himself into the leg space.

Outside the truck, Paul heard a door open and close. Very close. Footsteps crunch-crunched over concrete, growing louder as they approached the truck.

"Sorry," Sergio whispered as an itchy, moldy-smelling blanket settled over Paul. Sergio tucked the blanket around him, and Paul found himself feebly hoping his ass wasn't hanging out behind him. The blanket itched wherever it touched Paul's clammy skin, and the air trapped under the blanket heated with each careful, quiet breath.

The door slammed, jarring the truck and momentarily shutting every other sound out of Paul's hearing in a metallic explosion. Sergio's footsteps meandered around the truck and joined the other pair, which crunch-clomped towards the truck more lightly than Sergio's.

An old women's voice, hoarse with age, yet strong and willful exclaimed, "Marty, dear. Come in. Come in."

"How are you, Sary?" Sergio mumbled. His voice sounded respectful and very polite, almost losing the accent to which Paul had become accustomed.

"Not so bad, but seen better."

Sary sounded kind to Paul. The complete lack of nervousness and tension in Sergio's voice also reassured him, even if Sergio was using a completely different name along with a more sophisticated sounding voice. Sary sounded grandmotherly and kind, but Sergio's new persona, which for Paul amounted to a costume and mask, worried him. Paul couldn't think of many reasons why people chose to hide who they really are.

"It's been a while," Sary said.

Both sets of footsteps began to walk away from the truck, displacing small scratchy stones.

Paul felt dizzy, soaked in sweat and mystery beneath the old blanket. He had to fight the urge to jump up and ask questions, to ask Sary to take him in. She probably had air conditioning and TV and a refrigerator. Paul's temperature rose. Thoughts of coolness and comfort tormented him. Swimming pools and ice cubes. He wondered how many people died like dogs trapped in cars on hot days. The voices grew fainter, drifting away from Paul's hearing into the traffic sounds that hummed through his darkness.

"What do you have for me?" Sary asked.

"Statues. Got me a good General MacArthur."

"Oh come on, Marty," Sary laughed. "No one buys that old World War II stuff anymore. Most adults don't even remember the difference between MacArthur and Harry S."

"He had a good face. I like to carve it. The pipe is challenging too, to get it just right."

"Marty, try another face."

The door opened and closed leaving Paul alone with his pounding heart, stuffy breathing, and the soothing hiss of the engine cooling. General MacArthur, Paul thought. This is what Sergio or Marty or whoever carves. He had never given it a thought before, but he supposed the man must carve something. Why not those tacky old statues travelers used to buy on the roadway. They still do, thought Paul, astonished by the deep pull of cheap tack on the highway traveler's sense of want. He imagined Sergio carving up Jesuses and John Waynes and Sitting Bulls and all the other iconography of western American myth.

When the hot air finally became unbearable, Paul pushed his head out of the blanket's suffocating cocoon. The scorched summer air felt cool and almost refreshing for a few short moments while he gulped the fresh air and battled the profound sense of isolation and aloneness that seemed to well up whenever he couldn't hear or smell Sergio nearby.

Paul despised the vulnerable feeling. He always felt independent before the darkness settled over his eyes. The untethered astronaut sense of helpless isolation pissed him off and with nowhere to go, the anger was always on the verge of turning from desperation into panic. Major Tom to ground control, Paul thought, trying to focus on the old song rather than the helplessness and dread that never seemed to get too far away but rather was always a constant presence lurking in the darkness like some invisible beast waiting to swallow him whole.

The door opened again, and Paul pulled the old blanket back over his head. His muscles ached from being folded into the floorboard, and he wanted to sit up and look Sary in the eye. Hear her in the ear?

Paul listened to Sergio and Sary's steps approach the truck. A low rumbling, clattering sound preceded them. The sound, a cart of some kind, needed oil on its squeaky wheels. All the sounds—cart rumbling and step crunching —stopped towards the back end of the truck. A mild shudder rolled through the truck's frame as the tailgate slammed open, then a metallic thud as weight—Sergio's most likely—landed in the bed of the truck.

"Here can you get these?" Sergio called.

"They may be old ones, but I still got all my muscles," Sary laughed in an admonishing way.

Scuffling movements rocked the truck and successive thuds indicated heavy objects settling on a support of some kind. Paul guessed they were being placed on the rumbling squeaky sound that had come to rest. What a sighted person might call a pushcart. To Paul it was a rumbling squeaky sound at rest. He wondered if he would have to adjust his whole vocabulary.

"Beautiful, Marty. Beautiful," Sary mumbled.

"You like them, then." Sergio sounded pleased with himself.

"That MacArthur will be here a while, but those Jesuses, they look better every time. Them and those Kokopellis go fast. Had some old lady buy one for her church up in Dallas, just recent," Sary said through sharp intakes of breath. The statues must have been heavy; Paul could hear Sary's breath straining as she took them from Sergio and set them on the cart. He wanted to touch one of the statues. Feel its texture, shape, and size.

"What about these?" Sergio asked.

"The howlin' coyote... umm, yes. Indian chief, no. Still got me one of them. Sort of like ol' MacArthur, y'know? Nobody remembers who he was." Another mass banged onto the cart and settled. "I think you got yourself into a rut. You oughta try something new. You've been doing the same ones for years."

"How many you sold?"

"Most of them. Except these two, like I said. Got some cash for you, though. Round about one-twenty or so."

"Good enough."

The truck heaved upward as Sergio's weight left the bed and landed on the asphalt with a clumsy thud.

"Heard the news," Sary asked in a knowing-the-latest-gossip kind of voice.

"What's that?"

"Some kid killed one of the county cops."

Paul's stomach twisted while trying to do a flip. His heart beat faster. The temperature under the blanket topped four hundred degrees. Paul experienced a whole new kind of hot, number thirty-five, as Darwin's dangerous world snapped at him from the darkness that suddenly went from being oddly soothing to a place as full of malicious traps as kind strangers.

"Cut off his head, too, I hear," Sary concluded the tale of the deranged schizo drug freak Hell's Angel who was tearing up Armbister, raping the women and pillaging the ranches.

Sergio coughed and shuffled around on the concrete. Paul hoped Sergio was sweating as uncomfortably as he was.

"Painted his hands blue, too," Sary remembered. "Some kind of meth cult thing. Biker ritual or some such."

Paul wanted to shout the leaking pen incident to the world. To proclaim the trivial mistake and therefore claim his innocence, his case resting upon a faulty pen and indelible blue ink. He wanted to set the record straight on that if nothing else. Dammit. Sergio needed to get himself in the truck and away from the kindly voice full of questions and suspicions. Needed to get them out of here.

"That so," Sergio responded quietly. After a considering pause, he added, "Weird."

"Yeah, anyways—" Sary stopped abruptly. As if silenced mid-thought.

Paul's heart sank as he imagined her taking a glance toward the cab of the pickup. In Paul's mind, Sary (bright and sharp) noticed an old blanket covering an oddly shaped form in the footwell of the passenger seat. Venga aquí, Sergio. Let's go, man, Paul thought, wishing Sergio and he were telepathically linked.

"You getting out of here?" Sary asked, thankfully abandoning the previous train of thought.

"Yeah." Relief sounded in Sergio's voice. How in hell could Sary miss it?

"Here you are," Sary said.

Crinkly paper exchanged hands right outside Paul's window. How could she miss him this close? Paul's shoes started to melt in the heat beneath the blanket.

Sergio's invisible weight took a heavy step and then another.

"Marty," Sary said causing the steps to stop.

A shift on the gravelly pavement.

"Yeah?"

"Who you got under that blanket?"

Paul tried to flatten himself even more against the rubber floor. He felt like a scared cat trying to become one with the floor. As if the floor could absorb his mass and Sary would say, 'Oh, never mind. It must just be my imagination. Silly me.'

"Don't ask me no questions," Sergio whispered. He sounded like a ghost. His voice almost blended with the soft breeze blowing outside the truck.

Paul heard a distinct threat in Sergio's voice and imagined that Sergio too must feel trapped and cornered, but would fight like a healthy cat. Paul's heart hammered in his chest. He hoped that he and Sergio and Sary would all walk away from this peacefully and soon.

The pushcart wheels resumed their squeaky rumbling on the asphalt.

"Marty," Sary began without losing her friendly tone as if she assumed Sergio was just being melodramatic. Perhaps he was, Paul thought. He couldn't see Sergio, and he certainly couldn't read their friendship. "You know I would never—"

A sickening dull thud preceded a surprised yelp from Sary. Something hit the ground with a crack and the cart silenced.

Paul's stomach seized up. He tasted peanut butter and stale beer. His only thought was to help Sary. He threw the blanket off himself and with certainty that surprised him pushed the door open in a frenzied scramble out of the truck. He formulated no plan, but he couldn't hide while Sergio killed an innocent old lady.

While hurrying out the door, Paul's foot caught in the blanket, twisted, and brought him down, chin first, onto the concrete. His teeth clacked together, and he felt a burning fire race up his face.

Knee twisted and skinned on chin and elbow, Paul shook the blanket off and stood clumsily, holding still and listening, like a drunken statue. He listened for guiding sound, the sonar ping needed to regain his bearings.

He gave Sergio ample time to clock him. He waited.

Finally, Sergio calmly asked, "You okay?" to which Sary responded that she was fine, although her voice betrayed much confusion and a little pain.

Paul turned towards their voices. They were to his left. He wasn't even facing them.

"Help me get this damn Jesus off my foot."

Sary grunted and one of the wooden statue masses landed on the cart with an angry thud, which rattled the cart's wheels. Paul groped behind him and found the smooth metal of the truck. He slinked towards it as if he could just hide and pretend he'd never been seen. Two sets of footsteps crunched towards him, one heavy and sure, the other favoring one of its feet. Paul took a few deep breaths. The relatively cool air outside the blanket felt good in his lungs and on his skin.

"I knew you were hiding someone under that blanket, Marty. Didn't know you had any friends though."

"I don't," Sergio said.

"Then who's this fellow who just banged himself all to hell in my parking lot?"

Paul rubbed his head. He felt a cruel headache boiling like a vent up through the nether regions of his brain. His chin stung, and he wiped at the blood that was slowly dripping off onto his filthy t-shirt. "I'm—"

"Arthur," Sergio finished, cutting him off. "Sary, Arthur. Arthur, Sary," he introduced.

"Pleasure."

Paul extended his hand, and it met a small wrinkled hand that gave a surprisingly firm handshake. He decided to uphold Sergio's illusion of names for the present. Questions could come later.

"Thanks," Paul mumbled somewhat at a loss for words.

"You're all tore up, now," Sary said.

"I'll be okay."

"Why are you in your underwear? What's wrong with you?" she demanded.

"No questions," Sergio mumbled.

"Why were you hiding?" Sary spoke the words slowly, enunciating as if speaking to a scared dog or a child.

Paul imagined his appearance: dirty, smelly underwear; sightless confused eyes staring at nothing; wild hair and unshaven face; cuts and bruises. He tried to concentrate on not moving his eyes so he would appear more focused and less mad. It felt unnatural and only served to jack his headache up a few notches so he gave up the pretense.

"You blind?" Sary inquired. "You are, yessirree I can tell. Took care of my daddy for eight years after he lost his sight. Long years, those, before he passed on. Same confused blank look like you got. Am I right?"

Paul nodded. What could he say?

"I took him in a while back," Sergio said all calm and friendly again, his voice only vaguely accented, his manner non-threatening. "Ran away from one of those homes."

"Got pretty far without being able to see didn't you? They don't have a home for blind folks within four counties."

"Dumb luck," Sergio quickly answered before Paul could get a word in.

Paul became aware of a vague floral aroma taking over the greasy machinery and gasoline smell that dominated near the truck. He liked the smell of Sary's perfume. It made him wish he were clean.

"Well now, I won't tell anyone," Sary said. "Those homes are death. Worse than prison if you ask me. Family should look after family, I say."

Paul wondered if Sary thought Sergio and he were family. Maybe Sergio had light skin or maybe Sary was arriving at a less traditional definition.

"He's my nephew," Sergio said. "My brother married an Irish lady."

Sary gave a sharp laugh and began pushing the cart. "Come on. I got something that might help. Clean you up, too."

Sergio took Paul's arm and gently led him forward, following the cart through the door.

"I run a consignment shop, Arthur. Lots of stuff. Some people call it junk, but I think there's not much worth throwing out. Everything can be fixed up, re-done, or born again to new purposes. I got an old cane you can take. Glasses too."

"You got a TV?" Sergio asked.

"No. Alls I would ever watch is football, and I just go over to my sister's to watch the games. I don't think too much of TV."

"That's good." Sergio said.

The inside of Sary's shop smelled of candles and old wood. Old things. Things that no one wanted. Paul guessed this shop to be the last stop in the lives of relics that great-grandchildren couldn't comprehend. They wondered why the old geezers had held onto this or that, and then they sold it to Sary. That was the way the shop smelled. The flowery aroma of the candles further upped Paul's headache until he felt his head might start bleeding. Instinctively, he touched his chin; the blood had started to clot. He wiped his hand on his boxer shorts.

"Sit," Sergio said and helped Paul onto a short stool. Paul's feet touched the ground with his knees bent at a ninety-degree angle. "Be careful, there's no back, and you don't need to take another spill."

"Thanks, *Marty*," Paul whispered.

"Shut up," Sergio whispered.

Sary rummaged amongst boxes of endless knick-knacks. Paul heard wood and paper rustling and Styrofoam and metal clink-clinking against metal as Sary pushed and pulled her way through the maze of sounds.

"Hey, let me touch one of your statues."

"Why?" Sergio asked suspiciously.

"I want to feel it. You know, feel it and try to figure out what it might look like."

"The way blind people do in movies?" Sergio asked.

"Yeah," Paul said. "It might work."

Sergio clomped off and quickly returned. He set a large wooden mass on the floor. The floor and wood met with a familiar hardwood sound that proved Sary had a real floor. Paul extended his hands and found a large log that stood on end, its top reaching almost to his knees. Paul ran his fingers around the log. The back was rough and natural. The thick ridges of the old bark stood out like mountains. Paul traced his fingers to the front of the log. In a large recess, hollowed out from the front, he felt a shape, smoothed with sandpaper. Paul's fingers wandered about the carved surface. He felt ridges and depressions. Thin lines and cracks. Holes and mounds. Slowly the shapes ordered themselves into a form. A face. The face had long hair and a short confusing mass of beard. The edges of the eyes curved downward, and they felt sad and knowing but were offset by a faint ghost trace of a smile, a soft smile, and Paul imagined that if he could see it he might not register it as such, so close was the face to frowning.

Paul was impressed with the feel of the shaped wood. The delicate carving work, so opposite to the clanging metal noises outside Sergio's adobe home. Paul knew the clanging must be the initial work of carving out the recess for the face.

"Who is this, Sergio?"

"It's a Jesus."

Paul felt Sergio had caught the essence of the Jesus story: a sad man, willing to die. "It's pretty good." His fingers traced the odd little smile-frown a second time.

"It ain't no Frisbee on a string."

Before Paul could respond to the slight, Sary clomped over to them, still favoring one foot. She walked louder in her shop. She was the boss after all. "Here," Sary said. She placed the glasses on Paul's nose and carefully adjusted the earpieces behind his ears.

Sergio helped Paul to his feet, pulling his unwilling hands from the statue. He wanted to touch it more, to take more of it in. He wanted to explore all of Sergio's statues. Instead, Sary pressed a long cane into his hands.

"Now let's get you some clothes. You look like a damn madman!"

12

Bouncing down the highway in Sergio's truck, Paul felt the sunlight blazing through the window scorching his dried-sweat skin, his pores still clogged with dust and the grease from Ernie's fiery griddle. He ran his fingers along the smooth cane Sary had given him. A leather strap at the top felt rough and smelled of old wrist sweat. The truck hit a bump, and the bulky blind man's glasses jumped forward on Paul's nose. He reached up and slid them back into place. He was happy for the secondhand clothes she had given him. The t-shirt was old and worn, the jeans a bit baggy, but he felt better, as if the clothes somehow completed him.

"We need to get us some food," Sergio muttered from the space to Paul's left, slipping back into his Hispanic-tinged accent.

"More peanut butter, right," Paul sighed.

"Other stuff too. I was running low when you came along. I don't eat just peanut butter, but it does last a long time without a refrigerator."

"I was hoping that was the case."

"We have to get some stuff for Doctor Jakes, also."

"Who is Doctor Jakes?" Paul asked hoping it wasn't some other wild animal that Sergio had taken pity on.

"He ain't no medical doctor, if that's what you're wondering. He's one of them that looks up at the stars. Got an old observatory in the middle of nowhere. Has trouble getting out so I pick things up for him. Go out about every ten days or so."

"You take care of him?"

"He'd starve if I didn't bring him up some food."

Paul nodded. Sergio's intrigue factor went up a few more notches. So far Paul had learned how he got his money and now he was meeting his friends, all so normal in a weird desert-hermit-outcast-from-society sort of way.

The truck slowed, the tires protesting with a soft squeal as they took an arcing turn off the road and onto a bumpier surface. The truck glided to a stop, and Sergio's door opened.

"What now?" Paul asked.

"Gas station. Got a little grocery here. I'll be back soon's I fill up."

"Should I hide?"

Sergio considered a moment. The wind outside blew gently, and a car raced by on the near highway. "Naw. Didn't work before. Just sit tight and don't stare at nothin'."

Sergio stepped out, and without his weight, the truck rose a few inches. Sergio grew larger and fatter in Paul's imagination the more he learned to decipher sound. Assuming of course he was doing so correctly. The door slammed shut with a metallic bang that stung Paul's ears, the truck shuddered, and then Paul was alone with the soothing drone of the highway.

Sergio's steps edged around the front of the truck. The gas tank popped open with a sweet ting, and after some clumsy bumping of metal on metal and a few clicks, a strong gasoline odor told Paul that Sergio was filling up. Paul listened while Sergio filled the tank. He didn't register the sounds of the tank closing, the nozzle being replaced, or Sergio walking away. He just knew Sergio was gone as if he had seen the entire procedure and hadn't given it a thought just as a sighted person might watch absently while a friend completed a small task. In the back of his drifting mind, Paul took comfort in the fact that he could stay aware of his surroundings while not having to pay such close attention to every tiny sound, every informative noise. He breathed a bit more easily, and some of the knots in his muscles unwound. Knots that felt like they had been part of him for days and even a few knots that had been with him most of his life began to loosen. Despite everything, it felt good to be out on the road with the familiar wind blowing in his face.

Paul listened to occasional cars race by on the highway and wondered if that was the highway he had taken through Armbister the first time. He listened to the Doppler shift as the pitch of the cars' engine noises jumped from high to low as they flew past, oblivious as their drivers to the stoic scenery that Paul could only imagine. He began to separate the car noises from the truck noises and was pleased as a picture of the highway developed, devoid of color but richer in sound and tonal texture than anything he had ever heard before. The faint odor of gasoline tickled the edge of his nose, and occasionally a car or truck, drawn like a predator to the gasoline smell of blood, would slow, stretching the high tone as it pulled into the parking lot and thus never achieving the low Doppler shift of a passing vehicle.

One vehicle, Paul guessed a pickup truck because the engine was too loud to be a car and it had a smaller sound and lacked the hiss of air brakes that gave away semis, pulled in and drifted very close to him before its engine died. The tires rolled a few more feet, and then silence caused it to disappear from his perception as if it had turned on some kind of science fiction cloaking device.

Paul forgot about the invisible truck in favor of the other highway sounds until a door slammed open and closed. Hurried footsteps passed in front of where he sat. One of the steps dragged a little bit. The steps stopped in front of the truck. Paul tightened his grip on the blind man's cane—he knew he was being watched. Come on, Sergio, he thought.

The footsteps hurried to Paul's right side. He heard the excited breathing before the voice started up. "Well, I'll be god-damned. Look who's got balls to come back around here," an unfamiliar voice gushed with a surprised yet disparaging I'm-gonna-kick-your-ass kind of tone. The voice tickled Paul's memory, but he couldn't place it. Imagination.

"Who are you?" Paul whispered.

"You don't remember me?" The voice laughed. The voice was arrogant and snide and tough sounding. It had a low gravelly texture. The voice laughed again. Probably at the confused and scared expression Paul knew he was throwing around. Usually one's own expressions are seen reflected in the eyes of others. Paul realized his were reflected in their voices.

The laughter was as mean as the voice, not polite and gentle like Sergio's, it sounded cruel—the kind of voice that picked pointless fights, the kind that sticks its nose where it doesn't belong and gets it broken. The jigsaw shifted and took more shape revealing Broken Nose, the guy in the background at Ernie's Joint, the crude guy who didn't say much but sure wasn't disappointed to see Paul in that diner —Paul the murderer. "I remember you, *Paul Reynolds*." The laughter suddenly stopped, and the voice's owner became transparent. The cars on the highway ran right through him. Probably counting his reward money, Paul thought.

"You ain't even lookin' at me," the broken-nosed voice growled. "You should look at a person speaking to you."

Paul ran back over the shards of memory that seemed intact and certain. Tried to see the faces of the men in the diner. The air near Paul's face stirred, and the pungent smell of sweat found its way to Paul's nose. He pulled his head back away from the smell and the moving air. He remembered the name: Joe… Joseph… *Joey*. Joey waved his hand in front of Paul's face, testing for blindness. Paul could guess which finger he held up.

"Stop it," Paul said. "I can feel you moving the air."

"Jesus H. You really are." Joey actually sounded taken aback.

Maybe he had a guilty conscience for picking on a handicapped man, Paul hoped.

"Hence the cane and glasses, smart guy," Paul said. His words demonstrated a bravado he did not feel, and he doubted Joey bought the phony courage.

"Shut up, dipshit. They got a mighty high reward out for you. They don't like it much when people start killin' the county's finest."

"Tell the guy who did it, then."

Joey laughed, but then the laugh disappeared almost as it started. "Man, we all figured you was gone for good. Shit, man, we hoped you were."

Come on, Sergio. Paul clenched the cane tighter as if it were the only thing keeping him from falling into Joey's hands. He imagined Sergio in the store, waiting in line or worse, bargain shopping through scant aisles of gas station groceries. White bread and canned chili. Light beer and candy bars.

He smelled Joey's breath in his face. He was close. Probably leaning into the window. His voice smelled minty-fresh, and Paul found himself envying even this guy who got to brush his teeth and take showers every morning.

"Takes balls to kill a cop. Bigger ones to stick around." Joey sounded impressed with his statement, as if complimenting himself instead of baiting Paul.

Paul's sweat glands worked overtime. He felt like a hot, sticky film was being pulled over his forehead and armpits.

"You smell like shit," Joey sneered.

Paul knew he stank. Knew he looked ridiculous in his secondhand clothing and old blind man's getup. "I didn't do it."

"Or you don't remember. You look kinda banged up. Like you crashed that old bike. Maybe you don't remember. Maybe you got the amnesia."

"I got lost," Paul responded lamely.

"Maybe I could—" A car eased towards them and came to rest what sounded like a short distance away. Joey stopped as soon as the car's engine cut off. To Paul, the car sounded like an intruder. An unwanted third party with whom Joey didn't want to share his thoughts. A door slammed and footsteps strode past Sergio's truck and away.

"Maybe I could help the cops find you again," Joey said, his voice lower now, almost whispery like cloth dropping onto carpet. "I think you better come with me. Get out, 'cause I don't want to have to drag you and make a big damn scene."

Every muscle in Paul's body twitched. They all wanted to explode, to lash out at the spiteful voice standing over him. To run. To fight. Every instinct in his animal brain told him to make a stand, yet he sat in the truck, paralyzed by fear. Fear of falling. Fear of coming untethered. Fear of going to jail without even knowing what had happened to him. He sat in the truck, clutching the worn cane in a terrific effort not to shake.

"Get out. Now," Joey ordered.

The door creaked open, and Paul's hands instinctively grabbed the handle and pulled it shut with a deafening slam. "Listen," Paul said as he locked the door and rolled the window up to a tiny crack to speak through. "You get lost. Get out of—"

"Or what?" Joey cut Paul off. "You'll kill me too?" Joey laughed that fast nervous laugh. He sounded like a scrawny guy tormenting a bug and feeling good about it. "You gonna cut off my head, too?"

A great thud rocked the truck. Something solid pounded against the cab where Joey's voice had been. The voice managed the words, "What the—" before all the air burst from its lungs. The whole truck shuddered and vibrated and even tilted. Joey gasped for air, and Paul understood that Joey was being held against the truck.

Paul rolled down his window. "What's going on?"

Two thuds in quick succession rocked the truck. Each thud preceded a strangled moan and a sharp intake as Joey struggled helplessly for air.

"Sergio?" Paul asked. He didn't have to guess. He knew. And he found himself suddenly more afraid of Sergio than of Joey.

"Shh," Sergio hissed from the same space in the darkness that Joey's pained breathing came from.

After two deep gulps of air, Joey finally managed a word: "Hey!"

Another vicious thud (fist meets stomach) silenced him and sent a gentle shock wave through the truck.

Immediately afterward, the truck shook violently. Sergio once again pummeled Joey against the truck, and Paul heard his head snap back against the metal of the cab. Paul felt nauseous. Listening to a beating was far worse than actually seeing one. Paul remembered Joey from the diner. He had looked like a scrapper. Paul's mental picture of Sergio suddenly grew several feet and gained a hundred pounds. Mostly muscle. He had to be big. And tough. No gentle giant, he, Paul thought with a tinge of fear.

A door slam caused Paul to jerk his head around to pinpoint its source. An engine fired up in the direction of the car that stopped Joey. The car pulled out, and its sounds joined the occasional traffic before fading into the background noise. Paul knew Sergio was administering a horrible beating and doing it very discreetly. Sergio knew exactly what he was doing. Like a god-damned surgeon. Joey's limp sounding mass banged against the truck. Paul wanted to stop Sergio, but he was afraid. Of Joey. Of Sergio.

"Who are you?" Sergio asked.

"Fuck you," he responded. "I'm gonna find you, you punk," he managed to say through what sounded to Paul like terrible pain.

Joey's teeth cracked together on impact from Sergio's large fist, a wooden tenderizer smashing into a thick steak. Paul wondered if Joey might have bitten his own tongue off. A second later, a body fell to the ground. A few moments after Joey fell (for there was no doubt it was Joey) and didn't move, the driver's door opened, and Sergio's weight settled into the truck. Paul rolled down his window slightly to hear Joey scuffling to his feet as Sergio started the engine.

Paper rustled and several paper bags materialized in the space between Paul and Sergio. "Keep an eye on these," Sergio said as the truck lurched into motion. "I don't want the eggs to break. I want some breakfast tacos tomorrow, and if there's any broken ones they're yours."

Paul felt for the bags and counted them. Four. He rested his arm across the tops of the sacks to brace them from being thrown by the jarring ride they were about to take.

"Sorry," Sergio said. "I shouldn't have said that. A hand is fine. Just keep a hand on them." The tires squealed as the truck slid onto the road. The sharp odor of burning rubber filled the cab for an instant before the roaring wind blew it away. "You're hot, my friend," Sergio mumbled, more bent on driving than talking.

"I noticed."

"Cop came inside the gas station while I was waiting in line. Came around showin' off a picture of you and askin' if anybody'd seen you. Don't know how in hell they got that picture unless you got a record."

"It's my license picture. They downloaded it from the net."

"The net?"

"The Internet. You know, the computer network—never mind." Paul couldn't begin to explain. It would only sound like science fiction—UFOs and little green men.

"Anyways," Sergio said, apparently uninterested in the mysterious net, "He shows me this picture and asks if I seen you. I told him, 'No I ain't seen him, Officer,' and he says—get this—he says I should just keep my eyes open. That was half the battle. I almost laughed my ass off, I had to hold it in."

Sergio finally did let out a laugh. "Man, that son of a bitch walked right past you twice. Once while I was givin' it to your friend." Sergio howled with mad laughter as the truck accelerated wildly. "Some cop! God, I feel great!"

Paul suddenly understood why Joey had stopped talking when that car drove up. Why Sergio had stopped his assault on Joey. Paul knew exactly which car was the cop, and he thanked his lucky stars that the cop hadn't glanced to his right as he walked past him. He felt drained—as if all the good luck he might possibly have been born with had finally slipped away and in slipping away, he became less lucky with each mile Sergio drove.

"I wonder if it might just be better if I turned myself in. That guy was after more than a reward. If there was a cop around he could just have turned me in there and retired. Whatever, I don't think he was going to turn me in. He wanted something else."

"I saw his eyes. He would have killed you. It's the eyes that tell all the stories about people. You should be careful where you step."

"I don't want to get found by someone who won't at least give me a trial."

"You want to get tried in front of some West Texas hanging judge where the DA is his cousin?"

"I can't hide out forever."

"You can't get found either."

"I remember him. He was some face among a group of guys sitting at a table when I got chased out of the diner. I didn't even talk to him. I hardly even saw him."

"He has his secrets. Things he believes in anyway. We all do. Whatever he gots against you, you ain't ever going to know."

Paul slumped against the door of the truck. Nausea and a car sick swell in his gut caused him to revolve slowly in his seat, swaying and wondering if he would suffocate or throw up. Sweat dropped from his armpits and ran down his sides. "I don't know, Sergio. I don't know."

"They haven't found me yet," Sergio said kindly. "'Course forever's still got a ways to go."

Facts and knowledge shifted, falling into place for Paul at a disconcerting pace, his own jigsaw memory almost put together, but now the shapes of other puzzles rose up, sinister and silent like holes in time. These were the puzzles that described other people. He saw how their isolated pieces fit into his own dark edges, so dark that not even sound or touch or smell could illuminate them as they did the rest of the world.

Paul let the truck bounce him back and forth, occasionally jolting him into the air as the engine roared. Faraway, below a hundred feet of noise, Paul could hear the faint bass thump-thump-thumpa-thump of the Tejano station on Sergio's radio. Only the bass notes were apparent. He tried to imagine the most diplomatic way to ask Sergio the next question, the question hidden all along, the one he always suspected he would have to ask or at least learn the answer to. It seemed frighteningly obvious. Sergio had beaten Joey up good—enjoyed it too. He was obviously hiding. Hiding so low he couldn't even risk an electric bill, yet he relished the thrill of dealing with an unobservant cop in a public place. All this and he seemed kind, at least to Paul. Still, Paul had no desire to be on the receiving end of those nauseating dull thuds and teeth-cracking snaps.

Taking a deep breath and easing his grip on the cane, Paul relaxed himself. "Who did you kill?" he asked with a too casual directness. Might as well have asked what was for dinner. Or what color is the truck. Paul hung in the interminable breach of tact. A truck roared outside Paul's air-screaming window.

"We're almost there," Sergio said.

The truck jumped off the road and onto loose desert floor that made it wobble and shake. The wheels tried to skid to either side. Paul groped for the handle. The cane fell from his hand and landed with a crinkly smack against the grocery bags. Paul's other hand tried in vain to keep the rocking sacks from capsizing.

The truck skidded to the left, and Paul imagined Sergio was moving much faster than the first time they had traveled the empty space between Sergio's house and the highway. In fact, the truck rattled and vibrated so much that Paul wondered if the shocks would be able to absorb the pounding or would the whole truck just give up and fly apart?

"Son of a bitch was trying to shadow me. I saw him just before we left the road."

Paul remembered Joey and found himself relieved that the reckless, angry driving had more to do with evading Joey than a reaction to Paul getting a good guess in about Sergio's past.

The truck swerved violently, lurching as the wheels re-gripped the ground. Paul flew forward and gave up trying to save the groceries. Expecting a horrendous impact, he braced his palm against the dash. Dust filled his mouth as if he were licking the ground, kicked up into the air by the mad tires. The entire atmosphere of the small cab became choked with metallic-tasting particles.

"He's gone," Sergio stated as the truck slowed. The wind howl diminished as the truck resumed its comparatively comfortable bounce-lurch-bounce across the broken desert floor. The accordions and guitars in the music now accompanied the forever repeating bass line.

Paul leaned back and coughed. Sergio coughed but not as forcefully as Paul. His cough sounded more like a gentleman clearing his throat.

"You dropped the bags," Sergio said.

"Sorry."

"Bananas might be bruised. Eggs broken."

Bananas. Groceries. Christ, Paul thought, what's the deal? Out with it. "You're hiding because you killed someone," now or never, Paul pressed. Bounce goes the truck, jiggling through the darkness. "You might have killed that guy back there for all I know."

"I didn't kill him."

"Not anyone?"

Sergio's foot thwomped against the brake, and the truck screeched to a dust-raising halt. Paul slammed forward, bashing his arms against the dash, which was dry and cracked and felt like old wood.

Sergio's body leaned against Paul. For the first time, Paul could feel how bulky—how massive—the man really was. Probably two-fifty, maybe even three hundred.

Paul's door opened and before a synapse could fire through Paul's neurons, the irresistible force of Sergio's rough hand bore down on Paul's arm and easily forced him out the door and into empty free fall for seeming minutes, hours—*is there time in space?*—before Paul landed hard on the planet of Desert Floor. New bruises and a nasty case of road rash added itself to Paul's ever-growing inventory of minor but irritatingly painful injuries.

Above his head the truck door slammed shut. Sergio must have pushed him quite a ways from the truck because the door sounded far away. Paul raised himself up on his sore arms, as a man doing pushups, when to his horror the engine roared, and the tires scrabbled away on the rocky ground. "Hey," Paul shouted as he forced himself to his feet. He moved too slow, as if in a dream or under water.

"Sergio! God Dammit! Sergio!"

Paul yelled until his voice was hoarse and his throat dry. He was yelling long after the rumbling engine of the truck dwindled into nothing and disappeared over the horizon of Paul's hearing. Then the sounds of the desert took over, and Paul found himself standing in the middle of an empty universe surrounded by scuffling wind and nothing else. Small bits of dust blew in the wind and burned Paul's raw skin. Nearby scrub leaves scratched against one another like itching fingers.

Paul turned in a small circle, searching for any kind of recognizable noise. A sound with a human pattern. He was a radio telescope searching the skies for alien signals, the repeating patterns that would signal civilization: voice, music, language, machinery. Any roaring highway noise or even Sergio's truck coming back for him. Anything.

"God damn you!" Paul screamed into the parched air. He yelled loud enough that his throat turned to sandpaper, so he forced himself to stop lest he tear his throat up worse.

He listened to his words echo back at him from some mountain that must surely be looming out of the nearby desert. Radio telescope discovers mountain planet. Human sonar. No good, Paul thought. He stopped turning. Every direction sounded exactly the same in the homogenous universe of darkness and desert wind. Unlike deep space, though, this one was hotter than a hell with two suns. He took a deep breath. And another. If Sergio's dark past were an oil field he would have struck it rich. Black gold. Texas tea.

"Shit," Paul mumbled over the pain in his throat, just to hear his voice again. It reassured him. Helped him feel less alone. Less lost. That was it. Lost. All along, since the bike crash, if not before. Lost since he'd left California. Now it was just more obvious. Now he couldn't ignore it. He thought about the untethered astronaut and realized he might as well be on the moon.

He wondered if he should walk or sit and hope Sergio would be back. He tried to remember the direction Sergio's truck had disappeared, but that knowledge was lost in the crazy turning search for guiding sound. Paul sat carefully on the broken ground trying to regroup and figure things out. The sun blazed down on him from high overhead. Paul felt the direction of the heat, and he knew when it got lower he would have a decent idea which way was west. Sergio had said Armbister was west of his place. Wait. Wait and walk into the sunset like an old cowboy hero. Maybe he could find Armbister, stumble back to town lost and crazed after days in the desert, but unlike ancient mystics from the Indian past, Paul had no visions. He didn't even have his camera, and he wanted to laugh when he thought about how the exposed film showing UFOs would give him an excuse for fleeing and staying gone. He saw a space ship and freaked out. They did experiments and blinded him. It was aliens that got him and held him and... Paul smiled grimly. He knew no one would ever buy it because he wouldn't buy it himself.

Paul fought to hold onto a faint string of hope. He wondered if the string of hope was really the python tentacle that still lurked on the edges of the darkness that grew ever darker the longer Paul went without being surrounded by the light of comforting sounds. If he were an astronaut, at this point he would bite the cyanide. He doubted the string would lead him anywhere he wanted to go.

With no sight or sounds to guide him, Paul was cut adrift on a permanent space walk in a radio sky with plenty of gravity to help him trip on rocks, but no up or down or right or left. No help and nothing but the bitter knowledge that he was absolutely on his own.

13

Three hundred sixty degrees in a circle, three hundred sixty directions—more or less—Paul could walk, and all of it exactly the same. He sat for a while and listened to the endless desert, seeing it with his ears and hoping that somehow one direction would distinguish itself from all the others. The sun still felt high, blazing in the black sky. Paul wanted to move. He felt dizzy from the heat.

Carefully, as an old man, Paul rose to his feet and stood. He inhaled, trying to find the crude oil smell hidden in the nondescript air, and he wondered if he was simply used to it or if the wind had shifted. He couldn't remember whether or not the wind had changed direction, and he wondered at the human tendency to go straight to hearing as the backup for sight. There were other senses. He would have to learn to use them too. The air smelled hot and stifling as if smells couldn't move or were all being smothered by the odorless wind that blew onto his back and over his shoulders. It provided no comfort from the heat, but only seemed to aggravate it like the opposite of wind-chill.

The direction I'm facing, I will walk in, Paul thought. The wind is at my back, good walking scenario like in the old Irish saying. May the wind be always at your back and the blazing furnace sun always low in the west so you can breathe the killing desert ether. Something like that. Paul reigned his thoughts back in. Focus on the problem at hand. Start walking. What the hell? He knew he was more likely to be found by strolling across an interstate than by sitting in the desert.

Paul scratched his head. Forced his grimy fingers through the greasy tangles of his matted hair. If he reached a road, who would stop? He knew he looked like an escaped con or some kind of psycho just over the fence in Las Cruces. He remembered the signs in the middle of nowhere advising motorists not to pick up hitchhikers, the only sign of the local prison. It made no difference since he'd probably walk halfway to the median and get creamed by a semi.

Paul put one foot in front of the other and shifted his weight. His body drifted through its first step over the desert floor. Paul stopped. He was no longer in the same place. He had propelled himself a short way through space. He took another step and jammed his foot into a rock. As he fell, he had time to realize he had fallen more in one day than he usually did in a whole year. When he landed and the dust settled, he laughed. Crazy, drunken-mad laughter rose up from his throat, which contracted and burned with each fit. Maybe this is the point a person breaks, he thought.

Almost as quickly as it came, his laughing stopped and was replaced by the eternal wind. Paul wished Sergio had at least thrown him the cane. He climbed back to his feet and dusted himself off. He hoped that the next time he fell (he knew there would be a next time) he would fall over a long stick, one he could use as a cane to probe the ground.

No cane. No stick. Paul slid one foot forward and swept it in a gentle arcing motion across the ground in front of him. Feeling for rocks, sticks, cacti, anything with the ability to send him careening back to the mercilessly hard earth. Paul deemed himself fortunate not to have fallen on a big thorny cactus or landed his head against a rock.

He brought his other foot up to the probing foot and found himself pleased to have taken a step. Just one small step for man (without any help from anyone and in a direction of his own choosing) and one giant leap for Paul, it bore the satisfaction of being a step taken without Sergio's guidance. For a moment, ignoring the fact that he was in the desert heat with no food or water or shade or weapons, he entertained the illusion that he could survive on his own, but Paul well understood his predicament, the immensity of West Texas. Nothing for hundreds of miles and in some directions thousands of miles except barbed wire, and he didn't even want to imagine walking suddenly into a barbed wire fence. He could almost as easily walk to the North Pole as the Panama Canal without once passing civilization. Here, he decided, civilization meant more than a billboard or aircraft guidance system.

It would be hard not to cross a road but at the rate of one small sweep-step after another, it could take him one long hundred degree and waterless week to reach a major highway. Or a minor one. Paul swept his foot out before him. It brushed a rock. Paul shifted his weight as he brought his back foot up to meet the lead. He smiled at the knowledge of having circumnavigated his first rock. He hoped he wasn't just paralleling the highway.

As Paul lifted his foot for another step, light flooded his consciousness. A flash burst through his brain—his darkness disintegrating like ashes before wind—creating a glare that blinded him with light instead of darkness. He doubled over in pain, clutching his head, but as the glare receded, an image formed in Paul's darkness: black and white, low angle, slightly out of focus and overexposed. He *saw* his sneakers and the broken desert floor and the gray rock he had just found his way around. His lungs screamed, reminding him to breathe. He knew he had just seen his surroundings. He tried to memorize the area, the three or four feet around him that he could remember from the image flash. It was too distinct—too exact—to be imagination. He somehow must have opened his eyes and looked around, but as the image faded he saw nothing more than black as with a slide projector when the lamp-glow dies and the projected image dissolves into the surrounding darkness. Paul struggled to see the last glimmers of the slide as its afterglow faded. He memorized the rock to the side and saw he could take several steps without hitting anything.

Paul started to take a step but stopped when he considered what he had seen. The image had a low angle, and he could see his shoes. As if he was looking at them but not down on them. In fact he knew his face was up. The image was not from his perspective, from his eyes. Where then? He wondered if possibly his other senses were creating an image for him out of what they knew and he was organizing it as a vision. Paul took a quick three steps remembering he had at least that much before the next rock. One. Two. Three and Paul walked straight into a furry mass that quickly scampered away. Paul froze. He bent low and flailed his arms about, searching for the creature he had just collided with. Paul stopped swinging and listened. Quick short breaths blew in and out just beyond his reach. Paul squatted and listened to the animal pant.

"Mercury?" Paul asked. "Is that you?" Desperate hope danced nearby, and Paul wished his eyes would pop open for another moment. He moved his arms about in the empty air as if to grab hold of a piece of hope if not the dog itself.

The animal moved, its panting breath drifting around Paul as its paws padded towards him. A warm tongue pressed itself against Paul's grimy face and licked his cheek. The tongue felt cool on his sunburned cheek, and Paul enjoyed the feel of the wind blowing on his wet face for the instant before the terrible sun absorbed even that fleeting moisture.

Paul touched the animal's head and felt her ears and muzzle, relieved to know for sure that this was in fact a dog and most likely Mercury at that. He hoped it was. Paul scratched her ears and stroked her coarse fur. He ran his hand down her head and gently clutched the loose skin on the back of her neck. Without letting go of his gentle grip on the dog, Paul stood. He had to stoop uncomfortably, but he decided he could walk ten miles in a slouch if she would eventually go back to Sergio—if that was where her daily rounds took her. Even that sounded better to Paul than dying of thirst or exposure in the desert.

"Ever been a seeing eye dog?" he asked. He felt relieved to have company—even if that company consisted only of a dog or a coyote or whatever the hell she was. Paul didn't care. The dog came to get him. Mercury took a slow pace, probably slower than her usual gait, and Paul took careful steps beside her, sweeping his foot and moving forward with her. Paul clutched to her for his life and soon lost track of the turns they took as she navigated through the containing darkness.

Paul guessed they had gone about two hundred yards when Mercury stopped. A charred smell floated where a fire had burned recently, and the distinct smell of gasoline hung in the air as well. Mercury shook herself and twisted free of Paul's grip. He listened to her trot a few steps away.

"You're lucky she likes you," Sergio said.

Paul stood up to his full height. His back ached from being hunched over even for the short walk back to Sergio's place. Paul faced Sergio's voice. Relief filled him. Then rage. He wanted to hurt Sergio. He felt small and humiliated as he imagined Sergio standing just a few hundred yards from where he had been lost. He imagined Sergio watching him fall and scream and flail his arms about. He imagined Sergio trying to stifle that ever-present laughter. And it was the damn dog that bothered to bring him back.

"You son of a bitch," Paul said even as relief replaced the terror of dying in the desert. He felt exhausted, and he wanted to just lie down and cry. He wanted to go to sleep and wake up from this nightmare. "Did you think I could survive alone? Did you want to watch me walk around in circles and finally die outside your door for your amusement?"

"I figured you'd smell me cooking dinner and walk towards the smell."

Paul waited for more. Sergio's weight shifted as he leaned against the truck.

"Why are you playing with me?"

"I'm helping you."

"Great. Thanks. I should take my shot on my own out there. Jesus! At least your dog is helpful."

"She's a coyote."

"At least she has a conscience."

"I lost my temper," Sergio said.

Paul wanted to run. Not to get away but to expend energy. To release the excess adrenaline that was coursing through his body like bitter nails. Only now did he notice its aluminum taste in his mouth. He felt nauseous. He knew it was excreted by a very real fear of being left to die in the desert, but somehow he knew he didn't need it now. Even with Sergio, who had proven himself dangerous, Paul felt safe. He took a deep breath and counted silently to ten. He felt like his whole vibrating body would soon shake a hole in the ground.

"You're as worried about being found as me," Paul said. "I took a guess."

"I've been out here by myself a long time."

"You're crazy."

Paul let his words float in the space between them for a moment, and then he turned and strode away from the sound of Sergio breathing and let his feet move him in the direction he thought he remembered the house stood. His foot jammed into something and with a mumbled curse Paul began, once again, the all too familiar free fall express journey to the ground. Before the anticipated impact could jar his head and burn his outstretched hands, he stopped and hung in mid-air, an acrobat stopped in time. Sergio's big hand pulled him by the arm and brought him back to his feet before releasing him.

"You'll be okay," Sergio said from just behind Paul.

Paul nodded and stood in his place like an errant soldier waiting to be dressed down by his commanding officer. "Here's the stick," Sergio said as he pressed the cane into Paul's trembling hands. "You had it right. You're just five steps from the house."

Unassisted but for the cane, Paul traveled the five steps and entered the cool relief of Sergio's house. He found his backpack on the table, and he dressed himself in clean clothes.

14

Sergio shuffled into the house accompanied by the sharp rustle of paper bags. He brushed past Paul, who was just zipping up his jeans, and set the bags down on the counter. Drawers opened and closed, bags crumpled and tore, and objects made contact with surfaces as Sergio put the groceries in their proper places.

Paul felt not only cleaner but also cool. The new clothes weren't grimy sweat choked and unable to breathe. They were also his own and that familiarity with the touch and smell of them made him happy. He felt new, and the cotton t-shirt felt like icy silk against his burned and raw skin. The adrenaline flame had dwindled, and Paul felt content to simply stand by the table and listen to Sergio move about in the kitchen. He could hear every movement. Every action. He knew exactly where Sergio was and what he was doing and could almost imagine the man doing his tasks, except the visualization had no face and the kitchen no shape, and in Paul's perception, Sergio became like a lone featureless dancer performing before a black curtain, certain of all his movements and executing them with practiced grace and rhythm.

Paul's hand clutched the table's edge so as not to drift off into deep space, though in this room he could quickly find his bearings unlike outside where agoraphobia now prevailed. Paul remembered once loving the outdoors. Now, he feared it.

Sergio's symphony of groceries reached its climax with the popping of beer cans that might as well have been the cannons at the end of the *1812 Overture*. He walked towards Paul and set a can down on the table. Paul moved his hand towards the sound and put his fingers around the can. It was cold. Almost icy, it seemed to burn his fingertips, a pleasant freezer burn sensation that he savored as he wrapped his hand around the can. The memory of cold had nearly abandoned him. He sipped the beer, and it ran cold and smooth down his throat. He was usually one to scoff at the major American lagers, but he knew this was a beer he would not soon forget. For being cold and nothing more, it was the best beer he'd ever had.

"Forgot how good cold feels," he mumbled before taking another sip and riding the cool pleasure wave down his throat. His voice sounded less hoarse now. His body less wracked. He took another sip and then a long greedy gulp, enjoying the dizziness of the alcohol washing over him and how it eased the terrible weight of his limbs.

Sergio moved, and the chair protested with a groan as it took his weight. He burped, and the smell of the beer belch drifted over to Paul and hit his nostrils as if Sergio had been standing in front of him. Only by the sound of the chair could Paul tell where Sergio actually sat.

"I killed me a trucker," Sergio announced. "Drove a semi, y'know—Drove it into my car and sent me to the hospital for a month and a half. Had to learn to walk all over again like a little kid. I saw guys in the war got shot up and had a easier time getting it back together. Took me a while. Truck ran over the centerline and nailed my car and killed my wife and my boy. He was all drunk and fell asleep or some shit."

"I'm sorry. That sucks."

"It sucked. You said that, man. It sucked rocks. I punished him myself, though. The courts wouldn't 'cause we was just a bunch of... spics... and this guy had a cousin who was some big lawyer from San Antonio and he got him off. Figured she—we—was all just a bunch of illegals or something. Elena was a Mexican.

"Shit, I was holdin' all his people together in Vietnam, and I come back to be pollutin' the gene pool. When he got off I went to his place and killed him. I killed him slow, and

I made sure he knew who I was. I got his blood all over me while I carved him up like a damn Christmas turkey."

Paul's blood ran cold as the beer in the can. An icy electric shiver coiled down his back and into his legs. He threw back another gulp of beer, swallowing hard. Some stories required beer for the telling and for the hearing. Sergio slugged the rest of his beer and crushed the can in a hard thunder of smashing metal. Another can popped open, and one of Sergio's long sloppy sips followed.

"Didn't take the law long to figure out who done him in. I did it just as soon as I got out of the hospital. I wasn't careful, either. I was way too mad. Too pissed off to know that guy would be out there again. Before he finally died, he told me he was shaping up. That he got into the AA. I thought he meant Triple-A, and I told him they didn't have no road maps that showed the way around Hell, which was were he would be in a few minutes.

"I carried him to the bathroom mirror and left a long trail of blood along the carpet. I held him up to the mirror so he could watch while I slit his throat."

No logic or words came to Paul, just recoiling in the sheer horror of the methodic killing coupled with the reverse voyeurism. He held his beer can aloft, hovering between his lap and his mouth. It was not unlike watching a man die slowly in the desert. His fingers crushed the can slightly where he held it in a nervous death grip.

Sergio belched. "The world's a better place, anyway."

"My God. My God. My God," Paul repeated.

"Never killed no one in the war. Ain't that a laugh?"

"Didn't they ever come down on you?"

"Yeah. A little bit. I hid good, though."

"And you're still hiding out. It's why you can't turn me in."

"Yes."

"Is this where it happened?"

"Near here. I came here to hide, and I been here thirty years or so, I think. They stopped looking a long, long time ago."

"And you've been carving those statues and trying not to exist."

"I wait for Coyote to take me away. He always comes with death."

Paul killed his beer and crushed the can as Sergio had done before setting it on the table. He licked his lips and tried not to imagine what Sergio did all those years ago. He tried not to imagine what Sergio might still be capable of, if only pushed hard or far enough.

He wondered about Coyote coming with death and shuddered at the recollection that Mercury came for him out in the desert. He knew Sergio watched the whole scene, and he wondered if Sergio might be alluding to it, preparing him for something horrible and soon to come.

And yet, Sergio didn't seem to be driven by any irrational bloodlust, rather revenge. Paul made a mental note to in no way anger his captor, savior, provider, friend, and demon.

"Can you get me another beer?" Paul asked quietly. "I need another beer."

Sergio stood up and shambled past Paul to the kitchen. He popped a can and set it on the table. Paul picked it up and drank half the can in one long guzzle like a college boy on a Friday night. He wondered what day it was.

15

Paul sat in the dirt outside Sergio's house. He listened to the steady wind blowing its tales in smell from faraway. The cooler night air cascaded in waves from the sky and brought relief after another brutal and eternal day in the furnace. Paul enjoyed the feel of the air and the stirrings of the night sounds that bounced about on the rocks of the old desert: an owl screech, a scurrying mammal, a lone birdcall, and a distant coyote yipping and yawing.

Nearby Sergio sat on the ground breaking small sticks and shifting rocks and wood in a primitive rhythm that to Paul became like the sound of ancient man taming the wild. It was a musical piece, a grand opus—*Creation of Fire*. The ancient sounds affected Paul like a tape of soothing ocean surf. Disrupting all, a fart released the pungent odor of lighter fluid that splashed on the wood and twigs. Paul scooted a few inches away from Sergio to avoid being burned when the fire ignited.

Sergio stopped the noise, and his mass settled. Only the peaceful shifting of the friendly wind and distant birdcalls drifted through the desert. A desert owl hoo-hooted.

"I never realized there were so many birds in the desert."

"What do you mean?"

"The calls… there's so many different species, different sounds, like that owl." Paul pointed in the direction he had heard it.

Sergio grunted. "I don't hear no owl. Don't like them anyways. Beautiful sunset, though," Sergio said.

"Tell me."

Sergio paused, probably to stare at the sunset and try to frame it in words for Paul. "Sun's falling behind some jagged old mountains. They're all poking up in a black silhouette, and the sky is sort of reddish with a little bit of purple outlining the edges of the clouds. Clouds look like… like… I don't know, painted cotton balls or something. Up in the east a star's just coming out."

Paul tried hard to imagine the scene Sergio had described, but the colors were washed out and faded as if some mischievous vandal had spilled water on the mental painting. "It's Vega," Paul said imagining the lone star gracing the sunset.

"What is?"

"The Star. Its name is Vega."

"Yeah?"

"Second brightest in the summer sky."

"What's the brightest?"

"Arcturus. It's the first one that comes out. It'll be lower towards the west." Paul waited for Sergio to find it.

"I'll be damned, there it is." Sergio laughed. "You know the sky pretty good. Better than me."

"I camp out a lot. Camped. I also think about space a lot. Like what's out there. What's still waiting to be discovered. I look at a lot of those Hubble shots, y'know?"

"Hubble shots?"

"It's a big telescope up in space. It orbits the Earth like a satellite. It sees things you can't see from here. From even the biggest telescopes."

"Amazing. I remember when they put the first guys on the moon. Crazy sons of bitches if you ask me."

"I'd love to travel in space."

"But you don't believe in space ships."

"Not UFOs."

"Too bad. Space is so big."

"I don't deny there could be life. Hell, there probably is, you know. If they haven't killed themselves off or anything. I'm just saying there's no UFOs that come to Earth with Pleaidian wisdom or experimental alien abductions and crap like that."

"Why don't you believe in it?"

"There isn't any proof, Sergio. Until there's some proof, and I mean real proof, I won't be convinced. It's idiotic."

Sergio absently hummed a few bars of a tune Paul didn't recognize, as if he was thinking about what to say next and trying to make sure he got it right. "Why do you want to go out of your way to mislead people then?" Sergio finally wondered.

"It's a check. I have to eat."

"It's weird that you try so hard to fake proof for something you say isn't true."

Paul leaned back on his hands and directed his face towards the sky. He wished he could see the stars. There would be millions of them out here, so far away from the blinding glare of big city lights. He could probably even see satellites and drifting astronauts, untethered and watching the whole world spin as they died.

"You want to believe it don't you," Sergio persisted.

"Come on, Sergio. Give me break."

"Everyone wants to believe in something."

Paul thought he heard a lecture coming on. He shook off Sergio's comment and fought back the nagging feeling that Sergio might really be a manifestation of his conscience. "I wish I could see that damn sunset," Paul said.

"It's gone. Sky's pitch black now."

"The stars are out. Can you see any satellites, Sergio? Or shooting stars. Tell me, please. I want to see them."

"Paul, my friend," Sergio said, "there is no such thing as stars."

"Don't mess with me," Paul warned. He heard his words and knew the threat was empty and feeble as it left his lips; a blind man threatening a killer who reveled in his work like a pig in mud.

With a match stroke and faint whoosh, an explosion of flickering thermal TV static warmth obliterated the edges of cold creeping in through the darkness of permanent night. The flames and the burning wood comforted Paul as the chemical lighter fluid smell burned off. Sergio laughed, and Paul hoped that it wasn't at him. "What?" he asked.

"In the Army they called this a white man's fire."

"A white man's fire?"

"Them gringos build their fires too big, you know?" Sergio laughed as he said 'gringo' as if there was something interminably humorous in his use of the word.

"So what's funny? Are you laughing at the poor lost gringo?"

"No. It's not that, really." Sergio laughed again. His deep laugh resonated pleasantly in the night air. "I ain't white, hombre." Sergio's laughter trailed off into nothing only to be replaced by the wind. The fire crackled and snapped, and Paul edged closer to the warmth.

"What's for dinner?" Paul asked. He dreaded more peanut butter and wondered if he could actually eat it. In answer, a paper bag rustled, followed by a squeaky tearing sound: metal straining to force open a can.

"Beef stew in a can," Sergio said proudly. He set a can on the ground. Paul smelled the thick meaty stew, and he began to salivate like a starving dog. Mercury trotted out of invisibility and padded towards the fire. Her musty dog-smell and soft footsteps preceded her panting presence. She smelled it too.

Just exactly like a dog, Paul thought, wondering if her tongue was lolling sideways from her mouth or if she was cocking her head to beg. He wanted to believe she was too proud. Her hoarse and patient panting rasped between him and Sergio. Paul felt a new admiration for the animal, and a predator besides, that got by largely without sight, smelling it's mental map of the world. Far beyond sonar and radio.

"Smells good," Paul said for both him and Mercury.

"Are you kidding me?"

"No. It does."

Sergio took a long, exaggerated sniff.

"Hmmmph," he snorted. "You got a good nose. It smells like dog food to me. Until you cook it anyway."

The fire crackled more intensely for a few moments, and Paul imagined Sergio pushing the opened cans into the heart of the fire. The coals glowed in his mind, but they glowed white and not orange because he couldn't really see them. He just thought of words that could describe them.

The warm smell of the cooking stew drifted through the air and entered Paul's nostrils. He smelled it the way other people might listen to music or watch waves break on a beach. When it finished cooking, Paul and Sergio ate straight from the cans, wrapped in damp rags. Neither said a word while eating. They just savored the cheap food like they had spent forty bucks apiece. The cold beer even took on a quality like fine vintage wine. When they finished, Sergio gave Mercury his can and let her lick it out.

"That was actually pretty good," Paul said, settling back, enjoying the warmth of the stew in his body and the tingling that still lingered on his tongue.

"It's only good if you cook it over a fire. On a stove it just tastes like dog food."

Sergio's can quit clattering, and Mercury licked her mouth with loud slurping glee. When she finished, she quietly padded away from the warmth of the fire.

"See you, girl," Sergio whispered.

"Where's she going?"

"To howl with her kin."

"You just let her go?"

Sergio laughed and kicked his feet out across the ground. "She's my friend. Not my prisoner."

"Like me, I suppose?"

"If I am indeed your friend."

Paul mulled the thought over. Was Sergio expecting an answer? Were his eyes, focused intently on Paul, awaiting a decision? Or was he lying on his back, careless and staring at the imaginary stars. Paul thought about other people he had called friend, and he marveled that no one had ever done as much and been so kind to him as Sergio. He had also never been more afraid of anyone. A beer can popped open and then a second. Sergio put an icy can into Paul's palm, and they each took a sip.

"Only one I have," Paul decided after a short deliberation.

In the far distance, an eerie yowling erupted. The high-pitched yip-yawing quickly excited similar noises, all with different voices, joined in the same canine song. Many times in the past Paul sat alone in the desert listening to the coyotes and the unsettling atonal music. They sounded like some hellish free jazz ensemble with no rhythm section and no sense of scale or structure. The shrill voices rose and fell, one atop the other, singing as one with individual soloing calls and responses punctuating the din. Sergio laughed as the howling grew louder and more urgent. More insistent, as if the musicians were playing from different set lists.

A magnificent howl erupted several feet from Paul. The force of the sound and the unexpected closeness of the coyote so startled Paul that he clamored to his feet. Once up, floating on his feet and barely tethered to the fire circle all the howling stopped. Paul stood alone in the dark night surrounded by the drifting wind and nothing else. Then he heard Sergio laughing.

"That was me," Sergio said. "You shouldn't be so edgy."

"Are you trying to draw them to us? I can't deal with a pack of coyotes."

"They were making fun of you. I just stood up for you. That's all. Sit down."

Paul sat. The coyotes kept howling but with less apparent enthusiasm. Their song settled as the pack seemed more and more interested in singing the same song. Paul still felt uneasy. It was as if Sergio had somehow silenced them or changed the subject.

"You think they were actually talking."

"Not like us, but yes." Sergio said. "I wish you could see that look you're giving me. Man, I ain't crazy but you spend enough time out here or anywhere and you learn things that can't be learned racing through on the highway."

"I've heard that."

"You don't have to believe that they or any other animal talks. But they do. You just have to listen right. Like you're tuning a radio to the right frequency."

"What do they talk about?"

"What everyone talks about. What we all talk about every time we open our mouths."

"I'm not following you."

Sergio sipped at his beer and then belched. He laughed and belched again like a little kid with a glass of root beer. "They are talking about death."

"Are they really?"

"Remember what I said earlier about Coyote?"

"You told me Coyote always goes with death. Because they're scavengers I guess. I think you meant more."

"The Great Spirit created life. Coyote, who is the trickster, he created death. It was part of a joke he played on the spirit. But death, you see, is a double-edged sword. Coyote's people have to die too. Now, they howl at night to lament their foolishness and also in a way to sing of their wisdom. It really depends on how you look at it. If it wasn't for death the world would be too full so Coyote saved us, but because people still miss their loved ones, and it is Coyote who is charged with removing the remains, no one gives Coyote any help. He became a hated creature and a scavenger."

"And I thought they just ate trash," Paul said.

"They do."

"Did you make all that up or read it in one of those Indian myth books or something?"

"I heard it." Sergio drank some more of his beer, and Paul did likewise. His hand or the fire or both had begun to warm the can. "Somewhere, once, a long time ago."

"You sounded like you believed it. But I suppose people believe stranger things don't they?"

"Yes." Sergio's can exploded and bounced on the ground a few feet away. Another one popped open, and Sergio set into his next beer. "I do believe it."

"It sounds like an old Indian myth."

"One man's myth is another man's religion. After all it's all just myth designed to tell a wider truth. A truth we can't see or touch or hear. There's something vast beyond our knowing, Paul. Things we can't understand or even relate to."

"You believe in the Bible too?"

"Of course."

"You killed a man. You could've forgiven him."

"Sometimes I wish I had," Sergio said. "I have a bad temper and a violent nature. It's up to me to control these things."

"Sometimes?"

"Yes. Other times, I wish I could do it again and make it last for thirty years so the punishment would fit the crime."

Paul sipped his beer for a few moments. He was fast becoming drowsy. This was the second round of drinking for the day, and he was already exhausted from his adventures in Armbister. "I can't get into it, man," he finally said. "I just look out for me, you know? I don't see any vast truths or anything like that out there. There's us and here and now, and that's about it. Seeing is believing; it's a cliché, but it's true."

"You invent belief for lots of people with your flying saucer pictures. They see and they believe."

"I'm smarter than they are, Sergio. When I see something, I know what I see."

"You don't see much of anything anymore. How can you believe much of anything then?"

"I guess hearing will have to be believing now."

Sergio laughed. "How do you know that I am not a coyote waiting to take you? If I haven't already."

"You're drunk."

"Ah yes, but so are you."

The orchestra of coyote voices rose up again in waves, swelling through the darkness as each creature's voice joined the cacophony and seemed to egg on its fellows in a symphony of sinister laughter.

"Don't listen to them," Sergio said. "They're just laughing."

16

Images erupt on the black nighttime canvas of sleep, images more concrete than those formed in the wakeful hours when the eyes are closed. A mountain silhouetted against the stars, hands clutching the rubber grips of handlebars. A flick of the wrist, the speedometer needle punches farther up the dial towards the triple digits. A mountain looms nearby, erupting out of the ground and into the stars like a piece of the night has been torn out by a shaky hand to reveal the utter void behind the stars. Lights flicker singly and in pairs on the long horizon, brighter than the stars but transitory as the bike blazes past them.

I notice none of these things so desperate am I to flee the diner where the shotgun blasts still ring in my ears. I hear them over and over, louder and louder, and each time the pellets fly closer to me, and I gun the engine hoping I can outrun the shot before it tears through my worn leather jacket and into my back.

The silver balls glisten in the moonlight as they chase me. Their whistling rises above the howl of the wind just inches from my protected face. I push the bike harder, and the wind rises to a screech as I twist the throttle. For a moment, I feel as if the throttle also controls the wind. I follow the logic around the corner and realize I must not be moving.

I steal a glance over my shoulder to see if the glowing, following shot still pursues me. Brighter than ever before, it gains on me. The pellets—there are two of them now—glow phosphorescent against the perfect night. There is ample light, but there is no source. I glance at the stalled heavens. No moon, but all the stars ever imagined burn fiercely above, and still the crazy shot glows, growing.

"What did you see?"

I wonder if I hear the voice or if it comes from within. Wherever, the voice is airy—female. The wind dies, and I know I am no longer moving. I hear my own ragged and trembling breath race in and out of my lungs as if I had run the distance from Armbister. My hand unconsciously grabs the brake. I feel my heart hammering in my chest and wonder if the shot, when it catches me, will ease the painful hammering. I watch the shot grow closer and wonder how to avoid being nailed by the most powerful shotgun the world has ever known.

"What did you see?" the floating voice persists.

"Lights," I respond as the whistling grows louder and more deafening. "Lights!" I shout to be heard above the terrible noise. I say the word as if I control the lights myself. A pair of yellow lights blinks on below the white ones like a second set of electric

eyes. A pair of blue ones appears above them all. The lights grow in intensity to match the whistling that now screams. I admire the perfect precision of the formation of the lights. The pilots must be very good.

Pilots?

"Helicopters?"

And if so, where then is the thumpa-thumpa-thump of the blades slicing through the air?

A wave of nausea breaks over me, nearly pushing the bike over onto the blurry concrete. I gun the engine, but the bike doesn't move. I look down to see that I am completely stopped and balanced on the bike. As if time has stopped.

The lights take briefly to the air, then settle back low over the land. Perfect formation.

"Space ships?" I ask meekly. Unbelieving. Frightened.

The voice inside my head laughs. "You're kidding," it manages to say.

A dozen bluish-white lights dance furiously around me. I can't tell if they are ten miles or ten inches from my face. Two yellow lights appear amidst the blue ones and order them all into perfect little orbits before they begin to recede into space.

The wind, an angry beast torn by machinery, howls.

"Watch out. A boat."

I jerk my head up in time to see a beat-up old ski boat left by the side of the road. The words Anne's Revenge *stand out in bold black letters across the stern. I watch in horror as the front* tire smashes into the letters. *The* tire explodes, wood splinters and cracks, and suddenly I am floating among the stars.

The broken desert landscape rushes by beneath me at a dizzy speed. I twist my body and stretch out my arms in a vain effort to stabilize my flight.

Stars fill my field of view, twinkling in their stately rhythms of perpetuity, and I relax a bit because the stars don't move. I feel as though I am now suspended above the earth. I study the long tail of Scorpius and the Sagittarian teapot pouring into the scorpion's tail.

I glance about for the strange lights but see only the strange light of the stars. I smile, finally feeling comfortable at having outrun the whistling shotgun shot.

"You hit that damn boat every time," the voice says.

The voice has even followed me up here.

I watch my legs clad in their dirty jeans, now bearing a fresh tear and a little blood from my exposed knee, rotate into view, and I feel as though I am standing upon the stars, running along the back of the Milky Way. I remind myself not to look up in case the ground should be hurtling toward me.

"I didn't see it," I tell the voice, feeling a little annoyed that my star run should be interrupted.

"It must not have been real, then. Same ending though."

I watch my legs twist out of view.

For a moment the stars are back, shining by themselves and then with a bony crack every single one of them goes out.

Sometime later, one by one, the stars re-emerge from the light-absorbing void. I lie on my back and stare through the cracked visor of my helmet. Scorpius is gone, and the morning stars now shimmer weakly against the sun's dawning glare.

A single yellow light appears and hovers over me. It studies me. I stare up at the light. I try to wonder what it is, to care that it is hovering, examining me, but I can't muster the resolve. I watch until it withdraws and then abruptly disappears into the silence of deep space. As soon as it disappears, I forget it was ever there.

The stars slowly disappear, their light fading in the celestial batting order of increasing luminosity, as light fills the sky. I try to make sense of where I am and why I am here.

I remember noise and lights and a boat.

I try to move my body. I struggle to achieve a sitting position.

A dog barks.

Everything turns black.

17

Mercury barked a second time and then scampered about in the dirt.

"Good girl," Sergio said as if encouraging a child. Sloppy gobbling from Mercury's mouth said she scarfed something down and thoroughly enjoyed it.

Paul felt the heat of the sun wash over his filthy skin. He stretched his toes and lay on the ground trying to remember the images that had appeared in his dream. They seemed more vivid than true memories, which seemed to indicate that his mind still possessed the capacity to see. Of course the narrative made no sense. He even remembered the colors, but he couldn't fathom the story they once painted.

Mercury ran back and forth. Occasionally, Sergio would tell her she was a good dog, and then Mercury would chase something. Listening to them play, Paul gave the air a careful sniff. Wood-smoke and fire and bacon and coffee and gasoline and crude oil and dog shit all drifted through Paul's nostrils, each smell conjuring a fixed image floating in isolation like paintings on a gallery wall. He separated each one and catalogued it and determined a general direction for each—except for the crude; it was everywhere. No, not quite everywhere, Paul realized. Just on the steady wind that eased through the darkness. Paul placed the fire (and food and coffee, Sergio and Mercury) downwind of him. As the wind rose and fell, the fire smells rose and fell in opposite time with the shallow gusts.

"Did you sleep good?" Sergio asked.

Paul lay still. He wanted to feign sleep a little longer. He was interested in the smells and sounds, and he wanted to know how they would change as the sun's heat went from a vague warming of the left side of his body to an all encompassing directionless blaze. Would the wind settle? Were there clouds that would block the sun? How would the wind shift in relation to the sun? It seemed to be blowing from the north, considering the sun's current easterly direction. Of course, the sun would be slightly southeast and not due east.

"You had your eyes open for five minutes and then you closed them," Sergio said. "Stop faking, man. I know a gold-bricker when I see one."

Paul shifted towards Sergio's voice. "I was trying to enjoy the sunrise."

"Want some coffee?"

"Yeah. That sounds good."

"I don't got no milk or sugar."

"Don't need it."

Sergio poured a cup of coffee. Paul listened to the liquid pour into a metal vessel, like a tiny waterfall, before Sergio brought it over to him. What Sergio put into Paul's hand was a soup can.

"Don't worry," Sergio said, "I washed out all that stew."

"That's okay."

Paul took a careful sip of the coffee.

"Thanks."

It wasn't too hot and he tasted no stew, but he did get a vague smoky aroma from the fire, which made the coffee so much better.

Paul sat cross-legged on the blanket where he had slept beneath the invisible stars (he had seen them!) and drank his coffee. The can was almost uncomfortably hot, but Paul enjoyed holding it. It felt like waking up, and he found it invigorating. He did hope, though, that it wasn't the can Mercury had cleaned. The sun's heat rose over his body, and before he could finish the coffee, he felt too warm to want to drink anything hot. Holding it was nice, but putting it inside him where the heat would have him surrounded was not a thing he cared to do. The heat seemed a malevolent enemy; holding it in his hand, he could control it. He set the can down having only drunk half of the coffee. His body felt clammy, clogged. He wanted to wash himself so he could sweat and make the heat of the dawning day less stifling.

"What did you dream about last night?" Sergio asked. "You talked in your sleep, and you screamed one time and even threw up your arms over your head."

"I don't even remember going to sleep." Vague recollections of dreams still clung to his mind like dampness to a drying sponge, but they were barely images. Mostly words to describe the images that had flickered in his mind through the night and that were now evaporating in the blaze of the pitch-black sunlight.

"I passed out, and when I woke up you were talking some kind of conversation. I thought you were talking to Mercury, but then I realized I was drunk. I went to bed. Didn't mean to leave you out here. Too drunk to drag you inside, though. Besides I didn't want to mess around with those dreams."

"What was I saying?"

"No sé, man, I don't remember. Didn't make sense."

"I don't remember either. It's kind of fuzzy." Paul strained to remember details. Small things. *What did I say?*

"I don't ever remember my dreams. Every night is pitch black with no sights or sounds or smells," Sergio said. "No people. Just blackness."

"Do you want to dream?"

"No."

"Why not?"

"See, I've already lived through everything once. What are dreams but what we wish we had said or done or hope we can say or do?"

"They're supposed to be like windows into our deepest selves."

"When you are old, like me, you will realize it is better to keep the windows closed."

Paul's mind wandered to weird thoughts about flashes of color and starlight flying in formation. He stopped breathing for an instant. *Flying? Formation?* He felt his heart drop in his gut when he remembered dreaming about the crash. He closed the window.

"You smell like shit," Sergio said. "I'm going to let you have my bath."

"Your *bath*?" Paul asked. His voice betrayed his filthy-skinned hope.

Sergio laughed. "You look like Mercury trying to get some bacon."

"I wouldn't mind something to eat, but I'd trade it for a bath."

"You can have both."

"Where do you get the water?"

"From the ice I got in town, so I could have some cold beer and bacon and stuff that spoils. After the first or second day, the ice is about melted, and I just let it melt the rest of the way in that old washtub I got. The water's freezing cold, but by noon or so it feels pretty good. I soap up and get clean."

"I can't imagine being clean."

"Today, you are lucky, then."

"My pores are so clogged I can't even sweat anymore."

"It is one of my pleasures, but I will give it to you this week. I'm sick of smelling you."

Paul smiled. His mind swam with the idea of cleanliness, of feeling cool and fresh. He wondered if any of his cuts and abrasions from the crash and many falls were infected. "When will it be ready?" Paul asked.

"The tub's already out. I poured the ice into it right as the sun came up. That's how I knew you were having deep dreams. The noise should of sat you right up."

The dreams. Paul had almost forgotten. He pushed them away again, dropped them into the deeper parts of his mind. He wondered if he was merely dropping a yo-yo. He filled his nose with the smell of bacon. It sizzled in his nostrils like a childhood fantasy of a perfect meal come true. "Can I eat?"

"I made tacos." Sergio shuffled towards the fire and scraped a pan. A few minutes later, Paul was eating a fat taco filled with eggs seasoned with black pepper and hot chilies. A strip of bacon lay in the warm tortilla. The food was not just good because there was nothing else. It was excellent of its own accord, and Paul tried to eat slowly to savor every bite. He knew once the ice was gone there would be no more bacon and eggs, just the gooey monotony of peanut butter and bananas and warm beer. Paul ate five tacos while listening to Sergio who sat nearby, whistling.

The hours it took the ice to melt into sufficient water in which to bathe seemed the longest of Paul's life. He felt every speck of dirt on his body, each unwashed scrape. He smelled sweat, wood smoke, spilled beer, older sweat. He ran his hands along his gritty face. He normally kept it shaven, but at this point it had been at least a few days. Maybe more. Paul couldn't remember exactly. He wanted to shave, but stopped and considered himself lucky just to be getting a bath after a decent meal. He felt like he was at some discount health spa. It was turning into a good day.

While the ice melted, Paul listened to Sergio work nearby. The fire smell burned itself out, and now the whole atmosphere carried the scent of morning wind and far-off crude. Sergio was hard at work. He grunted and mumbled to himself in his Spanglish as he fought what sounded like a heavy piece of wood. Paul couldn't hear what he was doing, except when he used the ax for the great clumsy chopping work.

The gentle chiseling taptapthwack and occasional echoing whoomk of the ax lulled Paul into a hypnotic state where he wanted only to follow Sergio's actions along sonic pathways that led to a place in which sight only mattered in a secondary capacity and truth could be felt in the vibrations of the air. It began to sound like some kind of avant-garde musical performance, and very quickly the ax work developed a rhythm that was occasionally interrupted by the vooomfa-voomfa of a saw producing a pleasant dusty aroma, which the wind carried to Paul's nostrils. It was like seeing lasers go off in accompaniment to a rock concert, the spectator so enthralled by one sense that he is shocked by the sudden stimulation of another.

For the detailed carving work, Sergio used a quiet knife, and at these times, it seemed to Paul that Sergio was happiest, because the grunting and mumbled curse words disappeared and were replaced by a contented whistling and humming of tunes Paul couldn't place. Occasionally, Sergio's hum would trail into a long, unbroken monotone, a single note rising and falling like an Indian flute.

Thoroughly entertained by all of Sergio's business, Paul never gave a thought to what Sergio might be carving. He did not care. The process itself so fascinated Paul's remaining senses, he didn't even try to conjure images to go with the sounds. He simply followed them. Images presented themselves only with increasing effort and difficulty, the pictures that he could put together never matching the quality of the sound. It was like watching a super-8 movie with a high-tech digital soundtrack.

Listening to Sergio work in the loneliness of the blank desert, Paul felt as if he had somehow tuned a TV to a strange new channel that showed unimaginable images and invited the watcher to partake. Tuned a radio, Paul thought, correcting the analogy. He marveled at how ingrained the sight sense was, that even without it, he could not describe his lack of sight to himself without resorting to visual metaphors.

"God Dammit!" Sergio erupted.

"What's the matter?"

"I messed up a bit..." Intense chiseling and rough sanding. "Damned pointy-chinned motherfucker!"

"Whose?" Paul asked even though he already knew the answer.

"Yours."

"Me?" Paul laughed, but he had guessed right. "Why me?"

"You've been sitting so still and quiet that it's been easy to use you for a model."

"My chin isn't pointy."

"Looks pointy to me."

Paul rubbed his chin. *Maybe…* "Who in hell is going to buy a carving of my face?"

"Nobody. You ain't no general, and you ain't no Jesus."

"Why do it then? I thought you had to do this to support yourself."

"I don't have to sell everything I carve. Sometimes I do things because it's fun. You know, it passes the time. Don't you ever just take pictures of something because it looks nice or it would make a good picture to hang on the wall or give to some girl you want to get down with?"

"No."

"You're kidding me." Sergio stopped working.

"Dead serious. I never just took a picture because it looked nice. I always did it for work."

"There's no joy in that."

"Why?"

"First of all, it would be monotonous to carve up Jesuses and coyotes all the time. Second, it would cause my talents to deteriorate. Every lump of wood would look like a Jesus or a coyote waiting to hatch and third, it would become like just a process and routine and my work would lose its heart."

"I never thought of it that way. I just took the pictures," Paul said.

"Of course," Sergio continued, "your work lacks heart. It is used to deceive people and bring confusion. Your pictures are taken without heart. That is why you could never give one of your pictures to a girl to get her to take off her clothes. Women see through shit like that, man."

"I know," Paul said. "I went out with a bunch of girls who were always real impressed I was a photographer. They always like to tell their friends that they were dating an artist. But most of them couldn't have cared less about my pictures, though."

"None of them like your pictures?"

"A few. The last girl I was with loved them. She hung copies in her apartment."

"She sounds like a woman with heart. A good woman."

Paul laughed. "She was a drug dealer."

"Was?"

"Is. I don't know. We split up. She OD'd, and I got sick of always having to worry. I took her to the ER and left her there."

"Did she love you?"

"I guess. Yeah. She did."

"You are a fool," Sergio said. "I would give anything to have my wife back. You threw away a woman who loved you. What kind of person refuses to help a person in need? People hooked on drugs are looking for love, help, and things like that. You must have been on drugs too."

"I smoke a little weed. That's all," Paul said feeling suddenly sorry for Shan. Sorry about Shan. "You don't know everything, Sergio."

"I know that if you found me lying in the desert you would have gone on by."

"That's not true," he said, hoping his face wouldn't betray the lie to Sergio's eyes. He floated in the darkness and the silence waiting for Sergio to say something. Even the wind stopped and seemed to hang on Sergio's response. Paul did feel guilty about abandoning Shan, messed up and lost in that ER a thousand years ago in California. Now, he even felt guilty about never taking a picture for fun or out of a desire to express an appreciation for the beauty of a natural world that he was now denied. The fact was glaringly obvious: Nothing had any intrinsic beauty or value unless it somehow profited him. He had always believed the opposite to be true of himself. *Damn you, Sergio.*

"I think your bath is ready," Sergio said.

Paul tried to read anything in his voice, but it sounded as flat and dead as Paul had ever heard it. Sergio walked to Paul, and with a firm hand attaching itself to his upper arm, lifted him and guided him a few steps from where he had been sitting.

"Take off your clothes," Sergio ordered.

Paul carefully stripped and tossed his clothing aside. The gentle wind caressed his bare skin, and he enjoyed the feel of it as it drifted over his body, airing him out.

"Step up," Sergio said. He guided Paul forward.

Paul lifted his foot and eased it down into the frigid water. Chunks of ice floated against his foot, and it took a moment for the freezing sensation to reach Paul's brain because it had to do battle with his whole sun-scorched body. Paul couldn't tell if the water felt good or not. It was painfully cold, but he knew it would provide great relief against the heat. Gritting his teeth, he stepped into the tub. The water reached less than halfway up to his knees. He stood in the water while his body tried to decide to shiver or relax. Slowly, his muscles gave in towards relaxation, and he took a breath.

"It's always real cold at first, but you get used to it. Then it feels good."

Paul smiled. He imagined he looked like an idiot standing buck naked in the middle of the desert in a tub of ice water. He didn't care. His feet felt good, and the sensation of pleasure worked up his tired legs and throughout his grubby body. He was a hiker refreshing in a cold mountain stream after a long day on the trails, a kid glorying in a summer swimming pool, a sinner submerged and reborn in a Southern Baptist river ceremony. He squatted down and forced himself into the water. Ice shards clattered against the metal sides of the tub as he sat. He shivered for a long time, but eventually the sun melted the last of the ice and the bath became less of an ordeal and more of a pleasure.

Before going back to his carving, Sergio gave Paul some soap and a rag, and while Sergio carved out his song in Paul's image on the block of wood, Paul cleaned himself head to toe. When he finished, he started over and scrubbed himself until his whole body tingled with the smell of soap and the electric feel of open pores and skin once again able to breathe. With the cold water surrounding his lower body and the sun heating his upper body and his thoughts, a question blossomed in the back of Paul's mind, very subconscious, but it grew and grew and grew. It became more insistent, and soon Paul had to put aside his other thoughts about water and cleanliness and woodcarving sounds in order to examine this new one. Of its own accord, the new thought opened the window. Paul's dreams came rushing back in as if they had never left the active part of his brain at all.

He realized he had had the dream twice. Not just last night but before, back in the murky haze of waking from the crash. He struggled to remember another way for things to have happened. Something else to distract him from the boat before he hit it. Something besides dancing UFO space lights. Something rational. The problem, of course, was that the memories of the lights were just as much a part of the puzzle as the other things: the camping trip and the diner and his picture on TV. Everything else had borne itself out like a hellish prophecy. Why shouldn't the lights as well?

Because, they can't be. Clearing his mind to make room for each word, Paul thought: *There ... can ... be ... no ... UFOs. I make them. I am dreaming my work. I went camping and shot the Frisbee the night before. My mind is confused; it is jumbling memories.*

But, the Contraption doesn't do what happened in the dream.

I animated it.

But, I only see it as a UFO in black and white on photo paper.

It was in color in the dream.

Men don't dream in color.

It was a memory.

"Sergio," Paul called out. The water was colder, and the sun no longer seemed to warm his skin as if a great cloud had grown between the sun and his body, a massive nebula, a presence unseen but clearly felt.

"What?"

"I remember the dreams," Paul said. "The ones I had last night. I remember. They weren't exactly dreams. They were more like memories."

Sergio stopped working. "What did you dream about?"

Paul hesitated. Telling Sergio would constitute an admission of insanity to himself. Of course, Sergio would buy anything so Paul took some comfort in that thought at least. "I'm not nuts," Paul said. "I'm not. I hope you don't think I am, because—"

"You couldn't be any more nuts than you think I am."

Touché. Paul smiled and a small self-effacing laugh escaped his lips. "I was dreaming about the crash and when I hit the boat. I think last night wasn't the first time I had the dream because I remember the boat having different names. I think it was called *Anne's Vacation* or something or other."

"*Anne's Revenge*," Sergio said. "That's the name of the boat. Maybe *Annie's Revenge*. I don't remember."

"Whatever. It keeps changing in the dream." Paul stopped and cleared his throat. He wanted to remember everything right. He splashed water over his sunburned face to help clear his thoughts. "Okay, the crash," Paul began. "I wasn't watching the road; that's why I hit the boat. I'm a better driver than that. The reason I wasn't watching the road is that I was watching the sky. The sky behind me and around me. There were these crazy—crazy... Jesus, Sergio. There couldn't have been."

"Couldn't have been what?" Sergio asked walking towards Paul. "What did you see?" A sudden change in the volume of Sergio's voice told Paul he was squatting very close by. He had Sergio's full attention.

"I saw lights, Sergio. These dancing lights that spread out and came together and flew in perfect formation, dogging me down the highway. I never saw anything like that. They spun and went over my head—I'm not crazy—They were out there.

"I watched them, and I guess I never saw that boat because I was so into watching the lights. I never ever believed in all that UFO crap. For God's sake, I know they're fake, but I saw them. I saw the lights, Sergio. I saw them. I saw them, and I crashed my bike because I was watching them because I couldn't believe what I was seeing."

Sergio exhaled slowly through his teeth. "Damn."

"I'm not crazy. I'm sane, but—dammit, there's no such thing as flying saucers," Paul said mostly in an effort to convince himself. It didn't seem to be working.

"Maybe you fell asleep while you were driving, and you just dreamed the lights. Maybe you were dreaming about them when you hit the boat."

"I don't fall asleep while I'm driving. Never. Besides, there's no way that could have happened. I was too wired." Paul forced himself back to the flight from Armbister. "I was getting chased out of town. I'd just been shot at."

"Maybe..." Sergio trailed off. It seemed a long time before he resumed talking, and when he did his voice was faint, almost a whisper, as if he was afraid anyone might hear his words. "Maybe the lights are what blinded you."

Paul thought about this. They didn't seem extremely bright in the dreams. There was that one that hovered over his head at the end, but it was far out in space and there was no way he was going to follow this down the road of experimental abductions. "No," Paul decided firmly. "They weren't that bright. It had to have been the crash. Some kind of brain damage or something. A bad concussion. That's why it's hard to remember." His words sounded like rationalization—excuses—and he knew it.

"You ever read the Bible?" Sergio asked.

The Bible? "What does that have to do with anything, Sergio? Don't get all preachy."

"I'm not. But have you ever heard of Saul? He saw lights in the desert. They confused him, and he didn't believe his eyes so he went blind."

"What happened to him?"

Sergio laughed a little. "They cut off his head. Changed his name to Paul first, though."

"Do you believe any of this?" Paul asked. "I'm not sure I do."

Sergio thought about it, and Paul wondered if he was trying to imagine the lights for himself. "I think you saw something," he finally said.

"What?"

"Could be space ships. Or God. Or, I don't know, it could be just cruise missiles. They have that big Air Force base up there in New Mexico."

Paul shook his head. No way. No God. No space ships. He tried to imagine which one was least plausible. Both options appeared equally insane. He supposed there must be space ships somewhere, though. The universe was vast and seemingly infinite and possibly there was more than one universe. Maybe someone had figured out how to travel through space and bridge the light years to come to earth and chase him down a West Texas highway in the middle of the night. That would be a good use of time and spacecraft. Could it be possible? Paul resisted the line of thought. Arguing with Sergio would make it easier. Maybe it was cruise missiles.

"There aren't space ships… and God? That's another matter. This was some kind of machine—I'm sure of that. I must be nuts because those are my memories, but hell, Sergio, that Frisbee *is* the space ship. It has to be explainable. It was a machine because the lights couldn't have been—in and of themselves—sentient. That would be insane."

"Either the world is insane or you are insane. It's up to you to decide which. The answer you find will guide your feet forever."

"I want answers, Sergio. I might not ever get my sight back, but I will know what the hell caused me to crash out there!" He splashed the cold water on his face again and ran his hands through his tangled hair. He had a mission, and that made him feel better. It beat sitting around listening to Sergio for the rest of his life. "I want to see that doctor friend of yours," Paul said, remembering the old man Sergio claimed to know, hidden away in his silent observatory, alone with long years spent staring through heaven.

"He's just an astronomer. He can't heal you."

"That's it, Sergio. That's exactly it; he watches the sky. He can tell me what is out there. What I might have seen. He's got to know what flies around out here or if it was some kind of atmospheric phenomenon like ball lightning or something."

"Okay," Sergio said sounding the slightest bit glum. Paul knew he wanted to run farther with the metaphysical explanations. Then his voice brightened. "I did see an issue of *Modern Psychiatry* magazine out there once."

"I'm not crazy."

"It's a very long walk."

"Why can't we drive?"

"I don't want to tear up my truck. It's my only way out of here. When that truck goes, I'll be cut off forever. It doesn't have many more runs left in it. I can't waste any."

"Fine."

Sergio suddenly burst out laughing. "You will have to keep your head about you." He sounded like he might rupture his spleen from laughter.

Paul didn't find the joke that funny.

"Oh, come on, it's a good one," Sergio pleaded.

Paul caved and laughed a little with Sergio.

When Sergio lost the humor of his joke, he sat for a long time next to Paul while Paul continued bathing. Finally Sergio asked, "Do you think it might have been a space ship?"

"It might have been," Paul finally admitted. "It really might have been." He regretted ever laughing at all those hicks and rednecks who claimed to see lights in the sky, who knew beyond any doubt that they were seeing the technological triumphs of the beings that dwelled beyond the stars.

Afraid that this is what he had seen that dark starry Texas night, he hoped someone would prove him wrong, give him an argument in the name of reason so he would never have to admit to anyone—especially not himself—what he saw. He needed a story that he could believe. If he believed it, so would others. Then he could go back to civilization and claim he hadn't turned himself in because Sergio, a madman at large, was holding him prisoner. He wouldn't want to hand Sergio over; he could point the cops in the wrong direction or something, but he did have a good story to explain his disappearance. He didn't want any harm to come to Sergio since he had been so kind. Then Paul remembered with a sickening knot in his stomach the beating Joey had received only yesterday.

18

The unbearable heat hammered against Paul's skin. He thought he must look like a boiled lobster by now. He was used to the sun but not so much that he never burned. The bath was nothing more than memory and illusion, and his skin again felt gritty from the salt left after the sweat evaporated. Sun-high and feverish, he wished he were still napping on the couch in Sergio's remarkably cool adobe home.

"It's gonna rain so we go now. Here's a banana," Sergio had said as he rousted Paul into the blistering dark day. Paul ate the banana and dressed. When he came outside he felt no sign of impending rain, no ozone smell, no increased wind. "Trust me," Sergio said. "Vamanos." And vamanos they did.

Paul pushed his feet forward, one after the other. The banana was three hours ago, and now Paul's stomach was growling. The bacon and tacos were a distant teasing dream, a mirage only the tongue could perceive. Sergio was rationing the water, which to Paul seemed odd if rain was coming, but as Sergio pointed out, in the desert everything may feel like rain and then it just leaves you in the dust, parched.

The cane tapped out a steady beat in front of Paul's shambling feet. It didn't take long for the beat to fall into time with the Tejano blaring out of the radio that Sergio carried on his back. The idea was that Paul would follow the music and tap his way through the desert maze with his cane. Thus far it came off well—two or three stumbles early on, but then Paul found the rhythm, and Sergio guided him wide around major obstructions.

The longer Paul went without sight the more acute his sense of sonar direction became. It surprised him that he could follow Sergio's winding course through the desert with such ease; he wondered that he could even stay with him at all. It seemed he was becoming some robot, an animal living on instinct; follow the sounds, follow the sounds. As the day wore on and the sun grew higher, never once falling behind a rain cloud, the air temperature skyrocketed. Unable to fix any location, because it all sounded like Tejano music and smelled of crude oil, Paul felt as if he was drifting in orbit, perilously close to the sun, a black hole sun that radiated immense heat and no light. No visible light anyway. There were all kinds of non-visible light if you defined it broadly enough—radio waves, for instance the ones that guided him; of course, the actual sound wasn't light, but its source was.

After four or five songs and a short break full of Spanish advertising, which Paul couldn't understand, he was ready for a station change. The music all sounded the same, as if only one band existed and the station simply played every album they ever recorded over and over and over. He kept walking. The stick tap-tapped along the ground in front of him. The music grew suddenly louder, and Paul stopped as the music shifted and walked towards him.

"You look beat. Here's a drink," Sergio said above the music. He shoved the canteen into Paul's hand.

Paul unscrewed the lid and took a long greedy drink that Sergio cut short, tearing the canteen from his hand.

"Easy," Sergio said.

"Sorry. I feel like I'm going to die. Like I'm in this dark furnace and I'm just stumbling around in circles or something."

"You got that right. My place is about twenty feet from here." Sergio laughed and barely managed to get his next words out, "You're on the Chihuahua Death March, man. I just march you around in circles around my place till you cash in."

Paul stole another quick sip of the lukewarm water before handing the canteen back to Sergio. The water left a bitter metallic taste, picked up from the canteen, in Paul's mouth. He wished he could rinse his mouth with something else to get rid of the irritating taste of the water.

When he stopped laughing, Sergio took a prompt and disciplined sip from the canteen and then screwed the lid back on.

"I still don't see why we can't drive."

"Because you're blind." Sergio laughed again.

"Oh, Jesus, Sergio. What's got into you?"

"Nothing, amigo, nothing." Sergio chuckled and took a deep breath of the burning black ether. "It feels so good to get back to nature. If you could see you would know that you could look around here and see nothing, not one thing to show that human beings had ever been on the Earth. Not even any jet trails, man. No indication."

"It must be nice, because I can't escape it."

"How come?"

"All I can smell is crude oil. That's a pretty sure sign of human activity."

Sergio sniffed the air. "I guess I smell it a little."

"I smell it a lot. It smells like shit."

"I wish you could know how beautiful it is here."

"I'm sorry. All I feel is heat. There's no scenery here in the void. Nothing magnificent to stand in awe of. Nothing to make me pause and wonder. Just this black space that I seem to be drifting through with no direction that I can perceive. Everything is the same in every direction, and my only lifeline back to safety is you. And your god damned radio. That's pretty damn shaky, huh?"

"I wish we could have taken the truck, but it's old, and I can't afford a major repair job. I quit driving out here five years ago or so. There's no roads unless you want to go on a six-hour ride. There ain't no real highway connection between Armbister and there."

"How public is this observatory, anyway?"

Sergio turned the radio down, and the soft blowing of the wind took over as the dominant sign in Paul's sensory input. He realized the crude smell wasn't exactly everywhere, but rather it rode on the wind like a bitter knight.

"It's private. Real old. This guy built it himself and sometimes rented time out but as more and more people came to the McDonald facility it just sort of disappeared. Forgotten when all the scientists started taking their business elsewhere. Too hard to get to for one thing and for another, everyone thinks Doctor Jakes is crazy."

"Is he?"

"He's old. He can't leave and doesn't want to anyway. I found him years ago when I was out exploring. I used to hike for fun when I was younger. He gives me money to bring things when I come. Does the same with some family and a few others. I don't know who, but he knows people with nothing better to do than drop in from time to time. I don't know where he gets his money, but he's got a stash."

"You never thought about killing him and just taking his money?"

Paul waited, but Sergio never responded.

"I'm sorry," Paul whispered, barely audible above the wind.

Nothing.

"I'm sorry," Paul said a little bit louder. He waited for Sergio to respond. He waited a long time. "Sergio," Paul called feeling slightly panicked.

"I am right here."

Paul nodded. He turned his face away from the direction of Sergio's voice.

"I'd have to be a real bastard to do something like that," Sergio said. "The thought never crossed my mind. It did, it seems, cross yours."

Paul felt ashamed to ask his next question. "Do you think he can help me?"

"I saw that magazine there once."

"I'm not crazy."

"Mmmm-hmm."

"What's with this 'Mmmm-hmm'?"

"Your eyes are fine. Just fine," Sergio said. "You just don't believe what you saw."

"How do you know?"

"I'm standing here looking at you. Really looking at you for maybe like the first time, and I notice your eyes are real small, but I remember they were huge last night by the fire. So if your pupils are dilating, then maybe your eyes work and your head don't. It's about what I'd expect from a son of a bitch who would steal from an old man."

The music grew louder as Sergio cranked the volume. The explosion of accordion and acoustic guitar noise in the desert obliterated everything within Paul's range of senses. Then the crude smell came back. "Listos?"

"How do I know you aren't just taking me out to shoot me or leave me out here so you can just watch me wander around and die?" Paul yelled.

"How do you know I got a gun on me?" Sergio called back, his voice moving away from Paul at a slow but steady pace.

Paul, tapping the ground with his cane, began shuffling behind Sergio. "You have a gun with you?" Paul yelled above the music. He just didn't know people who had guns.

Sergio laughed again. Paul followed him farther into the broiling uncertainty of deep space, hoping that at the end of their trek they would find someone who could help him. He felt like a character from the *Wizard of Oz* and began humming the tune to the Scarecrow's song, "If I Only Had Some *Eyes*." Of course, the wizard would tell him he had them all along. Maybe if he could believe in the flying ships. Truly believe, like a reborn Christian, then maybe (maybe, maybe, maybe) he would see again. He pushed such thoughts from his mind, dismissing them as foolish and vain. He hurried after Sergio and the steady umpa-thumpa-thump ump-umpa thump o the Tejano beacon on Sergio's back. Maybe the gun was just for mountain lions.

Another painful hour of hiking passed, and by the end of it, when they found themselves standing at the bottom of a creaky staircase after an uphill, two-handed scramble over loose rocks and prickly pear, Paul realized he no longer felt hot. Tiredness and the swollen pain of cactus needles and cuts on his hands blew the heat away like whispers on a thick breeze. With a foot on the first wooden stair, he bent over to catch his breath.

"We're almost there," Sergio announced. He clicked off the radio.

"How many stairs?"

"I don't know. Fifty or so. We're mostly up the mountain. You did it pretty good."

"Thanks," Paul gasped. "Christ, Sergio, I'm tired."

"Come on," Sergio said, taking Paul's arm and carefully guiding him up the stairs. Paul counted each step. There were exactly forty. He felt his feet press the wood, and his muscles burned hauling up towards the observatory. Sergio never released his grip on Paul's arm. He knew there was no railing, and he sensed the way was steep.

At step forty, they stopped on a landing. "It's real narrow and small up here so don't move none," Sergio said. "It's a hell of a long fall from here," he added.

Sergio pounded his fist against a heavy wooden door that seemed to rattle in its frame after each meeting with Sergio's terrible fist. The rattling knocks drifted out over the desert and ricocheted off the walls of the nearby mountains before they faded in long waves that stretched to nothing.

"Whazzit," a faint and gnarled old voice asked from some other dimension, just on the other side of the door.

"Sergio," Sergio shouted at the door.

The old door creaked open, and the smell of liquor washed over Paul as if he'd just opened the door to a room full of broken whiskey bottles.

"Who is this?" The crackly old voice asked. It came from a few feet below Paul and sounded irritable and gruff.

"He is a friend of mine," Sergio said in a hyper-friendly manner. Not like speaking to a child, but not quite like a cogent adult either. "His name is Paul," he added.

"Paul, eh? Paul. Paul," the old voice repeated, trying the name out and experimenting with different ways of saying it, different tones. "I new a guy named Paul used to work down the hall. Poor bastard had only one ball and it grew so big it usedter make him fall." The man erupted in soft wheezing laughter that slowly changed to a hacking cough. "Come in, Paul. How 'bout a drink."

"No thanks," Paul said. Sergio gently pushed him forward into the room, then stepped inside and closed the door. The temperature was at least thirty degrees cooler. Paul heard air conditioning and the hum of electricity. It sounded foreign and pleasing and relaxing.

"I'll put your stuff in the fridge," Sergio said.

Fridge? Paul thought wildly.

"What did you get me?" Jakes asked, following Sergio.

Paul followed their voices a short ways, then stopped at the sound of Sergio opening a refrigerator. "I got rum, tomato sauce, pasta, chicken breasts, bread and eggs. That gonna do you?"

Jakes laughed. "What kind of rum?"

"Mexican," Sergio answered.

"That'll do, I suppose. My sister was out here last month. She brought the good stuff, though. Puerto Rican," Jakes giggled.

"Can I have some water?" Paul asked.

"Hang on," Sergio said.

"What brings you out here to see me, Paul?" Jakes asked, suddenly turning towards Paul. When he faced him, Paul could smell the liquor on his breath.

"I got sidetracked."

In the kitchen, Sergio cracked ice out of trays and into some kind of container. Then one by one ice cubes tinkled like bells into glasses.

"Hah!" Jakes barked over the promising ice sounds. "That's what Sergio says, but I think he killed someone, else he's on a hell of a long sidetrack."

"He wants to talk to you about a few things. I told him you're a smart man. You know a lot of things." Sergio put a glass into Paul's burning hand. He drank all the water in one long gulp.

"Well, we should go sit down then. Come on. In here."

Paul and Sergio followed Jakes through a door into another room, which was even cooler than the previous one. The air conditioner motor was louder, and Paul could hear it rumbling behind a nearby wall. Soft carpet gave a pleasant spongy feel to each step, and Paul managed to navigate into the room with only minimal help from Sergio and one stumble.

"Sit down," Jakes said.

Sergio guided Paul towards a seat, and the three men sat down. Paul's chair was soft and comfortable, an old easy chair. He reached to the side and found the lever. With a gentle tug, he reclined with his sore feet up before him. He cracked an ice cube into small pieces, spitting most of them back into his glass, but leaving one in his mouth to suck on.

"What do you want to talk about? No one ever wants to talk, even Sergio's always in a hurry to get lost whenever he comes here to do his charity work."

"What do you do out here?" Paul asked.

"I live here. Got no use for McDonald. Fars I'm concerned alls you need is good glass and a working knowledge of photography—no computers—makes for lazy work. Everybody left. I stayed."

"Why are you still here, though?"

"I live here. Besides, I wanted to keep watching. I think I'm the only one who watches for the right things. I make my plates, keep my records. I'll show you some of my images later."

He doesn't know I'm blind, Paul thought in amazement. It seemed unbelievable. Maybe the room was dark. He didn't imagine he could pass for sighted after such a short time. "What are the *right* things?"

Jakes laughed his gurgling phlegm-tinged laugh. "End of the world."

Paul leaned back into the soft cushions of his chair as if falling into a deep hole as already shaky ground once again gave way to free-fall.

"It will be written in the stars and seen in the eyes of animals," Jakes whispered as if quoting some random source. "There aren't any wolves in these parts anymore.

Ever notice? They've gone. Sumbitches knew it was coming."

Paul shook his head. He wished he could communicate privately with Sergio. A glance or a shrug or something, but Sergio merely sat next to him breathing loud and otherwise invisible, content to let Paul work into the atmosphere of the crazy old man's mind without burning up or skipping out into deeper space.

"I thought the wolves were just shot and poisoned to extinction by ranchers."

"That's what they say, but there's no wolves anywhere, not just here. I haven't seen a wolf in thirty years. That's where it started. Wolves, coyotes, dogs even. They sense things that we don't see."

It was no use. Paul couldn't argue with this guy, but surely Sergio thought there was some use in talking to him unless this was just another of Sergio's elaborate and cruel jokes. High and mighty Sergio. Anger rose up through his body until his head got hot and achy. "End of the world, huh?" Paul asked.

"Not just of our world," Jakes said with the intensity of a man who knows all truths gleaned from a lifetime of wisdom. "All worlds. Our galaxy is winking out, star by star by star. All matter reverting back to its most basic building blocks. Beyond neutrons and electrons: quarks, muons, pi-mesons. The cutting-edge scientists in particle physics constantly find new and deeper levels, but the truth, the one they ignore or are too blind to see, is that all of it is unraveling. Coming apart so everything can be reborn. Reorganized. This is why they keep finding new levels of matter, but they think they're so goddam clever. So full of themselves with their smashers and accelerators."

Paul found himself growing interested in the old man with the wizened voice, his hypnotic tone somehow making the craziest ideas sound plausible.

Jakes laughed. "You take me for a madman. You must think I'm just some loon. Let's listen to the crazy man spout nonsense. Bah! The universe is not a slave to our sense of time, what I'm telling you about is real, not some scientifically worthless coincidence based on our mystical fascination with round numbers. They say the world will end in two thousand, but whatever year, we're close, so close to an icy eternity, devoid of heat and movement.

"The stars are really going out, Paul. Sergio doesn't believe me, but he is much too polite to say anything. Besides," said Jakes lowering his voice for whatever good it did him as if afraid the very walls might hear his words, "I think he believes all that supernatural gunk."

Sergio, who sat breathing loud beside Paul, uttered a good-natured grunt. Jakes laughed. Paul sensed the routine of this conversation that might have begun decades ago.

"Anyways," Jakes continued, "I'm not talking about accelerated red shifts or anything like that. Stars and galaxies are literally blinking out. Not explosively but quietly as if disrupted from the inside out. Poof! Gone."

Paul's felt as if his head were spinning on his neck in ever faster circles like some children's top the doctor spun just for laughs. How could he not know that I am blind, Paul wondered. "How fast is the universe unraveling?" Paul asked. He decided to play along until he and Sergio were free since the old man's sanity surely evaporated years ago. Maybe hundreds of years ago. "How much time is left?"

"Fewer stars every night. Stars in the farthest reaches of space disappearing, falling away to darkness and the waves of dying stars are coming closer, rippling towards our own like a great black tidal wave, snuffing out the light. Our own sun will one day—one day soon, I should add—be one of them. It will almost instantly decompose into quarks and electrons. No traces will be left except a very faint background radiation signal, a dying ember, if you will." The doctor paused, then mumbled, "similar to the one left by the big bang, but I expect something more towards the X-ray spectrum and…" Doctor Jakes's voice trailed off into unknowable scientific ramblings the nature of which Paul could not fathom. Jakes's knowledge surpassed Paul's own limited awareness of astronomy, and now the old man seemed to actually be mumbling in the language of math with all of its mysterious grammar and mechanics.

"It will be a shame," Jakes started, reverting to English and back to a normal speaking volume, "we won't be able to see it. We will of course decompose as well. Too bad. Night would last twenty-four hours per day, and within a few weeks, the oceans would freeze solid. Of course by that point all life on earth would be gone. Perhaps it is better to die suddenly and not witness the slow freezing of our world and all that we love and hate."

"What sort of proof do you have for this?" Paul stammered, trying desperately to find some kind of firm intellectual ground. Firmer than quicksand, anyway. Sergio laughed to himself, a gently rumbling engine next to Paul.

"You are a scientist, right?" Paul prodded.

"I know what I've seen. I don't need some hippie drifter to tell me things," Jakes said sounding politely defensive.

"What do you see, exactly?" Paul asked leaning forward into the booze horizon of the old man's breath. Jakes leaned back, away from Paul, as if ashamed that Paul could smell his breath. He settled into his chair. Paul listened to the two men breathe out of time. Sergio loud and rumbly, Jakes thin and whispery like a rain of feathers.

"Years ago," Jakes began and then paused as if trying to remember. "Years ago, I saw that the dimmer stars, the magnitude twenties were disappearing. I trained my scope at things that weren't there even though the catalogues said they would be. I searched the atlases and the skies, but to my horror I found things that weren't there. First extragalactic objects, Messier objects, galaxies. Going, going, gone. Then the stars—even here in our own galaxy. Every month more and more of them are gone."

"Doctor Jakes," Sergio cut in, "could you please get Paul and me some more water? It's been a very long day, and we are both thirsty." Sergio's voice had lost its Hispanic warmth again. Like a chameleon, Sergio joined his surroundings; only alone with Paul was he really himself.

"Of course, of course," Jakes said. Paul heard the effort of rising strain the man's voice and could imagine the difficulty of getting out of the chair and moving to the kitchen. He took the glass from Paul's hand.

"Thanks," Paul said.

"Thank you," Sergio said as his ice-chiming glass changed hands from his solid one to Jakes's trembling one.

The chingling ice rattled in the glasses, drifting away from them, borne on Jakes's slow and careful step, which sounded more like the sliding of worn slippers on carpet than actual walking. When the distant pop of the refrigerator, followed by its amplified hum, reached Paul's ears, he turned to Sergio. "Crazy, senile or drunk?" Paul whispered.

Sergio chuckled. "No. Maybe. Definitely."

"After all that you want to tell me this guy isn't crazy. He's all over the place. He makes it sound reasonable, but come on, Sergio. Don't tell me you believe this nut."

"He ain't loco, Paul."

Paul waited for more. In the other room ice fell into the glasses while Doctor Jakes hummed to himself.

"He isn't crazy. The fact is the old bastard is going blind. He don't trust the other scientists or the computers they talk about in the magazines with all the pictures. He thinks it's some big plot. All he has is an old man's set of eyes and they're deteriorating. He thinks the universe is dying around him, when really it's him that's dying."

Paul shook his head and slumped back into the soft cushion of the easy chair. At least the chairs were comfortable. "Good God," Paul murmured.

Sergio went on, "Understand, his life has been built around looking up at the stars. With each one that goes, it's like he's got one less reason to live."

"How old is he?"

"Nineties, I think. Sometimes he says he is over a hundred."

Water gurgled into the glasses, and Jakes began his long journey through the inky blackness of his observatory home to where Paul and Sergio sat.

"He thinks I can see," Paul said. "Is he totally blind?"

"Not quite. But he don't see much past the end of his nose."

"Doesn't he know he's going blind?"

"He refuses to accept what he can't see. Now that that fails him… what should he believe, Paul?"

Doctor Jakes shuffled up to Paul's chair, and Paul took the refreshed glass from his weak and trembling hand. Sergio took his glass and mumbled thanks. Paul sipped his water, enjoying the icy feel in his still parched mouth. The pungent sweet smell of rum filled the room as Jakes opened a bottle and loudly gulped. Sergio cracked ice cubes in his mouth.

"I have a question," Paul said.

"Ask." A small burp filled the air carrying with it a rummy smell that didn't go away when Jakes screwed the cap back on the bottle and set it on the carpeted floor with a soft, yet firm, thump.

Paul took a deep breath. "Ever see UFOs? Is there any such thing?" He blurted the question, quick and breathless as if saying it would sound ridiculous and he would somehow be off the hook by admitting his own ridiculousness right up front. It didn't work that way, though.

As soon as the question filled the rummy air, he knew he really wanted—no, he needed—an answer for the sake of his sanity. His own question dwarfed him and rocked his being down to the very core. He felt like a person watching the events of his own life unfold, knowing he had taken a wrong turn somewhere, but was still, impossibly, going in the right general direction. He hung on Jakes's answer as if the words of a blind and senile old drunk could one way or another tip the balance of sanity in Paul's favor. Were there UFOs? Was there any such thing? Perhaps, the answer wasn't exclusive of sanity.

"That's why I began studying the stars. The very reason," Jakes laughed without missing a beat. His tone sounded as if he understood Paul's thoughts and the depths of the question as Paul saw it. His voice betrayed that he understood.

"When I was a boy," Jakes began, his tone switching. He suddenly wasn't crazy anymore. He sounded pensive and serious. He continued, "I saw something I couldn't explain. Something I only had ever seen in comic books. A cigar shaped light. It just hovered for a very, very long time, right above me, like my hand above the floor, see—this was before they invented helicopters, mind you—and oh, it was quiet. As if it sucked all the sound out of the night. And then poof! It was gone, just like that.

"It was like it had never been up there above the trees. I realized that the moment it left, all the sound came back on as if a switch had been thrown. I was in the woods, up in Michigan, and when it left all the owls and crickets and frogs and katydids came back. It was as if they were all staring in wonder just like me. Like all their little animal brains knew just like my little boy brain did that something was happening for which we—none of us—had any explanation. I grew up and came to the desert where the night goes out farther than anywhere else."

Jakes leaned forward and Paul's nose recoiled from the fresh rum that drifted on his breath. "Have you seen one?" Jakes asked.

"I think I did. I think so. I think I saw one." Paul felt comfortable and at ease. The old geezer seemed to understand, and Paul's fear of being branded nuts by a lunatic evaporated like dew before the morning sun. "It was like you said, I got so wrapped up that everything else stopped and ground to a halt, and I crashed my bike. I was out for a while. It left my memory real hazy, and when I woke I couldn't see."

"But you see now," Jakes said.

"No. I don't. I'm blind—I can't see a damn thing. You talk about your disappearing stars, but they've already gone out for me."

"Yes, but that's just because you're blind," Jakes said kindly.

"What does it mean, though? Why can't I see?"

"Mean?" Jakes laughed. "Mean? It doesn't mean a damn thing. They're just running away looking for a safe home, trying to outrun the dissolution. Like we would if we had star ships. They certainly wouldn't have crashed their flying saucer wondering what in hell you mean. They are living beings like us. Just trying to get by.

"It is very, very arrogant for we humans to assume everything means something, every random act directed specifically at us. All that matters, Paul, is that we will be dead soon. Our species won't have the technology to get out before our sun goes. It's just part of the cosmic cycle."

Paul leaned back in his chair. He hadn't realized he had been leaning forward as if being drawn in by the insane gravity of the doctor's words. Now he felt discouraged as he listened to Jakes drift away again. "You know, Paul, all the matter in our bodies was made in ancient stars that blew up in supernovas before anybody ever thought about time." He stood up slowly in front of Paul and shuffled away a few feet. "Are you hungry?" Jakes asked. "I can make dinner. You could even stay a day or two."

Paul felt sorry for the lonely old scientist, a prisoner of age and a solitude he had inflicted upon himself by seeking to riddle out the meaning of a cigar shaped light. It was obvious in his tone he wanted them to stay. He wanted ears to listen to his ancient stories and confused theories. He sounded like he was begging. Did Sergio hear it too? "You know I never stay," Sergio said flatly.

Paul found himself wanting to stay. Not just for the air conditioning and the refrigerator but for other reasons that seemed vague and strange. Maybe it was just the cash he purportedly had stashed, but perhaps he too wanted to know and learn. And oddly, he wished he could do something to help Dr. Jakes as well.

"I know." Jakes said. "Dinner. You shall stay for dinner."

"Dinner would be fine," Sergio said.

Jakes stood up and shuffled back to the kitchen on his carpet sliding slippers, humming quietly to himself.

"I don't believe it," Paul whispered, half to himself, when Jakes was out of earshot.

"What?" Sergio asked.

"I don't know, maybe it is true. Space aliens. UFOs. Maybe I've missed it by being so caught up in manufacturing the proof."

"I don't know that there is one absolute truth," Sergio said. "It seems we choose our beliefs and make them real for ourselves."

"Sergio, I've sold lies for my living and betrayed everyone who was ever kind to me. I've never done a decent thing. Jesus, Sergio, what am I?"

19

Sergio and Paul kept their voices and their thoughts to themselves for at least the first half of the long walk back to Sergio's home. Walking home came easier. Their stomachs were full of spaghetti and thick meaty sauce. They were hydrated, and the night air had chased most of the heat away from the desert. The moment they stepped out of the observatory, long rolling booms of thunder appeared on the sonic horizon. Sergio commented that the far sky was flickering on and off faster than the booms and so the storm would be pretty harsh if it washed over them. For that reason, they took a different, less direct, route home that Sergio said would avoid getting them caught in the flash floods that tore like watery lightning through the bone-dry landscape. Paul didn't mind walking the extra hour to avoid that trap.

He poked the ground with the stick and silently followed the radio, which drifted in the darkness before him like a lighthouse beacon he could never reach. The usual desert animal sounds hid from the radio noise and probably also from the impending storm. They knew it wasn't wise to be out. Paul wondered how much animals did know and how much they didn't care about, just going through their lives. He wished he could live like that. Like Sergio, the violent ape.

The music clicked off and Paul froze in place, not wanting to go farther. "What's going on?" he asked the darkness.

"There's an arroyo, we gotta climb down and across. Only low point on this route home."

"How steep?"

"It's pretty steep," Sergio said as if calculating a difficult math problem. "I'll help you down," he finally said. "Give me your hands. Lock them with mine."

Paul did as he was told. Sergio's hands were hot and thick. He remembered the thuds they had dealt to Joey. Sergio guided him backwards until Paul could feel his heels hanging over the edge of what might as well have been the Grand Canyon for all he could tell. He wiggled his feet and sensed nothing but empty air beneath them.

"Take a slow step back," Sergio instructed. "I'll hold you and you can just sort of walk down backwards, like you're rappelling until I can't reach no more, then I'll let go and you should only drop three feet or so. It's clear down there."

Paul began to sweat despite the cooling air and increasing wind. "How deep is this gully?"

"About ten feet."

"You sure?"

"You have to trust me."

Paul nodded. Carefully, and not without a bit of nervousness, he stepped back and eased himself down the side of the gully. He felt Sergio hunch over and then lie down at which point Paul dangled in space. His feet floated in the air.

"Okay," Sergio said. "Let go."

Paul clutched Sergio's hands. He fought to let go. Part of him fought to hang on. His hands wouldn't release.

"You're tearing my arms off, man," Sergio pleaded.

"How do I know?" Paul yelled over the building wind.

"Trust me," Sergio said. His voice strained.

It did not come easy and never would, but Paul released his death grip on Sergio's wrists and dropped through limitless space an eternal three feet. His feet landed hard and flat on the sandy ground and a painful shock wave rolled up his body, vibrating his knees as it went.

Paul stood on the bottom of the gully, listening as Sergio scrambled down to join him. Rocks and dirt bounced to the ground until finally a solid thud indicated that Sergio was down. He stood up and dusted himself off, clapping his palms against his clothes as he did so. "I need to rest before we climb out. We'll wait here a few minutes," Sergio said. His voice echoed around the short walls of the arroyo.

"Why here? If it's going to rain, this could be a bad place to be."

Sergio laughed. "I like it here." His laughter trailed off as if he was preoccupied by something. "Wow," he whispered.

"What?"

"The lightning, man. It's just flickering and jumping around up there. You could read a book by it, it's so bright."

"Quite a storm, then, huh?"

"Yeah. Quite a storm."

"What the hell are we doing in an arroyo?"

Sergio gave a short laugh. "Taking a break. Here, have half of this candy bar." He gave Paul half a chocolate bar.

Paul put it in his mouth and chewed. It only made him thirstier. He wanted water. Not enough to fill the ditch, though. "Come on, Sergio, let's get out of here, I don't want to get caught in a flash flood. This is suicide."

"Who cares? What's a little death? I am tired."

"Sergio," Paul said, "what in hell are you talking about?"

"There is no sense in fearing something that is inevitable."

"Inevitable?"

"You heard me!" Sergio roared above the now constant collisions of thunder. "*This* is inevitable," he continued, but lowered his voice slightly, "I ain't gonna babysit you until I die. So it's inevitable that you need to think about seeing again or it will be inevitable that I will get caught. And I ain't goin' to no prison. No sir. So you must decide here and now if you will see or if you will stay here. You eyes are fine! It's in your cabeza—your head, man!" Sergio's voice grew quieter. "And if you stay then one more thing is inevitable. This wash will fill. It always does. Every big rain and this wash fills, and they will never find your body."

"Jesus Christ, Sergio. What in the hell's got into you? I can't help that I can't see."

Raindrops, fat and far apart, began to smack against the desert floor. Occasionally, one hit Paul's head or arms. He wiped at the water as if swatting away mosquitos.

"What's got into me? I look at you, and I start to get scared. I see someone the cops are looking for. They've forgotten me, but eventually they'll remember when they catch up with you. I brought you out here to see Doctor Jakes to maybe give you some perspective."

"Perspective?" Paul yelled. "On what?"

"Your brain works. You got something you can use. I don't want to be no babysitter!"

The thunder grew louder and in the far away, almost imaginary, distance Paul thought he could hear a faint but constant rumbling. At first he mistook it for thunder, but it continued and grew louder at a steady, slow and inevitable pace.

"The water's coming," Paul said.

"You could tell them you were going to answer their questions, but you saw a flying saucer. You freaked out."

"The water is coming!"

"Sink or swim!"

"Sergio," Paul screamed in frustration more than rage, "People don't believe this kind of crap. They lock you up for it."

"People see a lot of strange things out here," Sergio responded. A faint metallic click punctuated his sentence.

Paul's heart hammered against his chest when he realized what that click was. He had never heard it live, but he knew the sound of a pistol being cocked from a thousand movie soundtracks. Beads of sweat stood up on his skin and the fat rain, ever increasing, washed them away, down into his eyes and his ears. The sweat burned in his eyes, and he closed them against the pain. How odd, he thought, that his eyes should hurt. He wiped his hand across his face. The rain had begun to fall more heavily and the thundering wall of water, like an earthquake, drowned out the steady patter of raindrops on the ground. Was it better to drown or be shot? "I know you've got a gun,

Sergio, and I don't know if you can hear it or not, but that water's coming."

"It's okay. I can swim. I was a world-class swimmer when I was a boy. I won all kinds of swim meets." Sergio's voice sounded distant and far away. He sounded like a different person.

"Sergio," Paul yelled above the din of thunder and rain and the rushing water echoing up the wash. "You can't swim in a flash flood."

Sergio laughed. "I ain't gonna be no crutch, man. You gotta get up and go." He sounded like Sergio again, but it still didn't seem as though he was fully aware of his surroundings.

"I can't go without your help. Not yet. We need to get out of this ditch together."

"I don't want no ties. No worries, man. I want to die alone and not in some prison. You just tell them that I held you. You tell them I wouldn't let you go."

"The water's coming! I can hear it!"

Paul turned in several directions as if he might run off at any moment. He tried to sense the best way to run. It was pointless. He could hear where the water was coming from, but he didn't know the direction of the closest side or the easiest way up. The gully could have twists, and Paul would simply be trying to outrun the inevitable torrent bearing down on them like a hellish train.

Two gunshots, in quick succession, tore through the darkness and froze Paul in the midst of one of his terrified turns. A blue arc spark tore through his mind after each shot. When the last notes of the last shot reverberated against the walls into silence, Paul could barely stand he was trembling so badly. It seemed hours before the realization that he had not been shot came. Then his heart sank. If Sergio had shot himself, he would be just as dead, by drowning though and not by bullet wound.

"Sergio," Paul asked.

After a long and terrible pause:

"Yes."

"Why did you do that?"

"I couldn't do it. I couldn't."

"Jesus Christ, Sergio. What's got into you? Do you want to kill me or you?"

Sergio laughed, sounding relieved more than anything else. "It's not in my nature. Not anymore anyway. I ask you though, why should I not kill you?"

Paul rubbed his eyes, as if he could rub the blindness from them. He took several gulps of the wet air. "I don't know," was all he could manage to say.

As Paul said this, Sergio pressed something cold and metallic into his hands. Paul fumbled with the gun until he was certain it wasn't pointing at him. "I can't shoot a gun. What do I want with this?"

"I don't need it," Sergio said. "You might."

"For what?!?" Paul screamed over the din of everything bearing down on them at once as if the entire world had reached its end, and now there was only the last blow to extinguish everything.

"Mercury?" Sergio's voice shouted in sudden amazement.

"What?" Paul asked, confused and near panic.

"Here it comes," Sergio yelled. He grabbed Paul's hand and yanked him backwards, all but pushing him up the slippery wet side of the gully. This wall was only seven feet or so and not difficult for Paul to scramble up. He heard Sergio struggle behind him, trying to force his bulk up the wall. The roar of the water drowned out the night and the darkness. Instinctively, Paul spun and dropped, grabbing towards the sounds of Sergio's huffing breath and scraping hands.

He clutched Sergio's wrists and held on as tight as he could. His knuckles hurt, and when the flood rolled through, the water tried to break Sergio away like a kite in a hurricane wind. Paul clung to Sergio as the gravity of the water worked to pry him loose. Sergio grew heavier and more massive, the water soaking into his clothing, tearing at what it claimed for its own. Determined that Sergio would not drift into space, Paul found it amazing and invigorating to be the tether holding his friend and tormentor to the earth and not the other way around.

Somehow, Paul was no longer drifting. The noisy darkness still surrounded him, and he wondered if he would ever see through the gloom, but he had found a planet. The drifting feeling was gone. This new planet had gravity, though its sun did not radiate in the visible wavelengths; for Paul, the sun would always be some kind of strange radio star—a star shining in distant Tejano frequencies as the water tore at its bearer. Paul clung desperately to keep Sergio from sailing away into the swirling angry void of the flood. Inch by inch, Paul struggled, pulling Sergio against the momentum of the water and towards the bank. Paul fought to tune out the thunderous noise of the water tearing past them. Using his last reserves of strength, and panting like a worn-out dog, he gave a mighty pull.

But Sergio was gone.

20

Rain continued to pelt the earth, growing softer and softer, gentler and gentler as the thunder drifted away. Paul wiped his eyes, whether of tears or rain he wasn't sure. For hours, he sat, unable to hear or feel anything save the pounding of heart and lungs. The desert had turned to mud, and now it surrounded him and seeped into his clothing and shoes. Eventually the night stilled and quieted. Paul listened hard for the now familiar sounds of the desert, but the sudden violence of the storm had scared everything away and left Paul alone in a wilderness of silence.

Paul got on all fours, feeling the ground to learn the location of the arroyo that had washed Sergio away. His hand bumped a metallic object, and Paul put his hand around the gun. He felt the shape and the firm texture of the weapon, and careful to point it away from himself, he pointed it above his head and squeezed the trigger. The sound came as sunrise to a sighted man, full of energy and hope. He listened to the echo in the far distance, reverberating back to his ears from distant rocks, hills, mountains, unknowns. With sound, he was not alone. Hoping he could draw someone to him, he almost fired again, but then decided he may need to save shots in case he stumbled upon a mountain lion.

He stuffed the gun into the back of his pants as he had seen countless TV heroes do and continued his search for the edge of his world. He knew that they would have proceeded away from the wash to get to Sergio's place, so he would walk away from it. Just before the edge, he found his stick, which he must have dropped when Sergio threw him up to safety. When he found the edge, he backed up a few paces and then stood. He probed the ground with the walking stick, tapping it about. He then extended one foot, feeling about with his toes, and finding no obstructions or hindrances in his path, he planted his foot and brought the other up to meet it.

He stopped counting his steps at one hundred and five. He could feel the early morning fire on his skin. The air was dry, but Paul felt humid as the sun steamed the sweat from him. He knew desert animals and survivors sought shade during the hottest parts of the day, but he knew no way to find any so he decided to keep walking until he couldn't, banking on the hope that perhaps someone might see him.

He tapped his stick ahead of him and brought his foot up next. Then the other. He repeated the rhythm for hours, avoiding cacti and rock and thorny mesquite bushes with a dexterity that amazed him. He never once fell, and the rhythm of the stick tapping the ground and his feet swishing up behind became increasingly automatic as the daytime nightmare heat drank him, lapping away all that was not exhaustion.

He knew the sun had reached its zenith because it was all around him, had him trapped in a tomb of heat from which there was no way out, only through. Everywhere the darkness seemed to glow with strange color, yet there was no vision involved. Tap. Tap. Tap. Step. Tap. Tap. Tap. Step. Tap. Tap. Tap. Step. The steps came slower and still it grew hotter. Tap. How many miles had he walked? Tap. The sun had come up long hours ago on his right. Tap. He would have no idea of his direction until many hours later when the sun began to set. Step.

Voices came on the wind, blowing now from what Paul believed to be north. Probably the wind that brought the rain, and now Paul wished it would bring more. He stopped and listened. The voices rode down the north wind, calling now, then singing, then sometimes even repeating his name.

He knew one voice—a woman's—was Shan. Blowing in from some California ER, where he left her long ago.

"What?" Paul yelled, his voice hoarse and echoing across the barren soundscape. He stopped walking. "What?"

Wind. Laughter. Wind.

Paul shook his head and kept walking. "This can't happen," he mumbled to himself.

Shan walked along beside, saying nothing, but keeping step. He could hear her breath and smell the incense perfume she always wore. "Why? Why did you leave me?"

"I don't know," Paul said. He shook his head trying to get rid of the hallucination. "I just didn't want to deal, you know. It's not me."

"I needed your help."

"No you didn't. You didn't want it."

Shan laughed. "Poor Paul. Always so free, so sure."

Paul stopped. "This is not happening!" he yelled every word to the blazing atmosphere that suffocated him without remorse. He pulled the gun from his pocket and fired it into the sky. The explosion erased everything: the laughter, the voice, the smell. Only wind remained, drying his burned skin.

"Dammit," Paul muttered, tucking the gun away. He resumed walking, and decided to ignore the soft footsteps that trailed a few steps behind him. There was no way they could be real, and so they were not there.

For long periods of time, the footsteps would stop and disappear, but they always reappeared, rising out of the wind, a mirage for the ears or a ghost bent on haunting him quietly into madness. Occasionally, Paul would stop and swing his stick in all directions, but the feet stopped as well, and he never hit anything. "Because there is nothing to hit," Paul mumbled to himself. A part of him observed that his speech slurred. He kept walking. Tap. Tap. Step. Pause to catch the breath. The pauses grew longer and more hopeless, and when the wind finally relented to the point that he could no longer feel it, the temperature seemed to rise even higher, leaving Paul with a headache that made thinking a labor not worth pursuing. The cane, a foot, another. Paul resumed his hopeless death march across the bleak and silent desert, wondering if he was getting nearer to anything, and quickly losing interest in caring one way or the other.

The sun burned holes in Paul, and sweat turned to salt burned his skin. He kept walking, but he forgot why or where he was going in his android's march towards an oblivion he could no longer fathom or even believe in.

"Paul?" Sergio asked.

Paul stopped walking. "Sergio?" he whispered into the wind that was now blowing again, though less steadily and with a slight shift to the west that brought back the crude. "Sergio?" he asked again.

"Yes?"

"What happened?"

"What do you mean?"

"You were washed away. Weren't you? In that flood?"

"I suppose so," Sergio said.

"You aren't really here then are you?"

"No, I guess not."

Paul nodded and started walking.

"Maybe, though," Sergio called after him, "I never was. Maybe it's all a matter of what you believe."

Paul kept walking until he could no longer hear Sergio's gentle laughter.

Exhausted and dehydrated, Paul stopped walking when he noticed that the sun had dropped to a point near the horizon. Paul eased himself down to a sitting position, and he leaned on his stick. He muttered a string of obscenities and wished for some way he could at least tell his parents what had become of him. He wished Sergio had shot him. He removed the gun from the back of his pants and held it in his lap, feeling its cool metal and wondering if he could just put an end to it. Hunger, thirst, starvation, and animals would all be much worse than a quick shot in the head. He held the gun for a long time and listened to the wind blow night around him. Eventually the footsteps that had pretended to be with him all day began again and moved into the distance, blending in with a twilight desert now rich with sound.

Paul despaired as even his hallucinations walked away from him, leaving him to die alone and forsaken. Paul held the gun in his lap, fingering it and carefully tracing its unfriendly, yet oddly reassuring, mechanical texture. Now he was untethered, and he held his cyanide in his lap, ready to be used and bring on a quick ending before he was eaten by the cold loneliness of his own space.

He relived the sequence of events that had led him to this point. The cop, the diner, Sergio, Jakes, Sergio, Sergio, and Sergio. Thinking of Sergio made Paul feel ashamed for wanting to pull the trigger on himself. Why should he do what Sergio believed to be wrong? Ultimately that was it; Sergio believed it would be wrong to kill him.

Paul cleared his mind until he found a peaceful space in which he could just sit and listen to the music of the desert night come alive with hunters and prey, song and magic. Far away, he heard an engine. Maybe a truck. Then it was gone, and Paul was alone again. Then another truck, going the other way, and Paul smiled knowing that where there were trucks there would be highway. He would find it the next morning, and he would be saved. But for now, exhausted from the mad torture of the walk, he didn't care. The air cooled, owls hooted, coyotes howled, and snakes rattled. Paul listened, entranced.

It was still nighttime when Paul woke. He sat up. An engine rumbled, closer than the highway he had heard earlier. Paul grabbed his stick and jumped to his feet. The engine was far, but he heard it traversing far left and right, miles from him, but on an erratic path. Such as on a search, Paul hoped eagerly. Paul fumbled on the ground for the unused gun, desperate to call the attention of the driver. He fired the gun, once, twice, three times into the air, savoring each explosion and thrilled by the way it left the desert in frightened silence for a few brief and powerful moments. Paul waited and listened. The engine had stopped, the vehicle now invisible.

A return shot sounded in the distance. Paul fired again into the air. Another shot returned, this one closer. Then another, and to Paul's terror, the ground exploded not too far from his feet. He jumped up and ran headlong into the desert, away from the shots. Another erupted in the near distance behind him, and another—farther away as he put space between himself and the place where he had been— told him that he was running at a dangerously fast pace. Soft footsteps glided over the ground, sometimes just behind him and sometimes ahead, but never far. At least my fantasies are staying with me, Paul thought.

Far behind him now, the engine started and plodded its way toward him before it cut off again. Paul kept running into the wind alongside the terror-imagined footsteps and oblivious to any obstacles that might get in his way. His luck held for a good distance, but then came a rock to grab his foot, and Paul fell into the earth with terrible velocity and the anger of gravity long defied. His arms broke his fall enough that his face was protected, but the wind flew from his lungs, and he lay on the ground gasping like a landed fish pulled from the ancient seabed that now was desert. He knew he couldn't outrun destiny for long, and like that fish he was caught.

The strange footsteps circled around his imagination, as a guard on watch or death spiraling closer he did not know. When his breath came back, he just listened. Somewhere, a man yelled hoarse obscenities into the night air and occasionally fired a weapon. Paul was pretty sure who the man was.

He wanted to run, but he was too exhausted, too hurt, his adrenaline spent. He imagined himself running into the wind and through the desert to a strange freedom that was different from anything he had known before and from which no one could remove him. The clarity of the vision filled Paul with peace because he believed he could see himself charging into a new world, one of bliss where he would be free of all worry. Flying into this awesome desert of the mind, Paul eventually passed out face down on the desert floor, clutching his stick in one hand and the gun in the other.

Somewhere a dog barked.

21

My motorcycle races away from Armbister, and I huddle in the saddle, nervously casting glances over my shoulder down the black highway. Occasionally, I glimpse the lights of Armbister, but they disappear as the road dips beneath my tires.

I search about, scanning the landscape for small feeder roads on which to hide. I know I will be followed. I know they are going to come after me because they chase people who kill cops. The cops chase them. Ahead of the cops, though, will be the ones who really did the killing.

"Come on," the strange voice says inside my mind.

The voice is not of my mind—it is not me speaking to myself —it is another entity altogether. One that shares my mind or somehow manages to communicate directly with it.

Behind me, not far down the eternal highway, the roar of a heavy-duty pickup truck asserts itself in the otherwise quiet night, its lights blazing and tearing holes in my mind.

Memories—illuminated—reorganize, perspective shifts, and I remember things: a chase, a truck, a desert shipwreck…

"Hurry!" the voice persists.

Lights bounce about the highway, casting sweeping electric glares in my rearview mirrors. "Why?" I ask. "I'm safe here." I don't know if I actually yell the words over the scream of my engine or if I think them. Either way, they are heard.

"You aren't safe. You must get up and follow me."

The front tire of my motorcycle smashes against the boat, and once again, I leap off the motorcycle seat. The heavy engine screams behind me, but I leave that behind as I arc high into the moonless night sky, shooting through space near the speed of light.

Ahead of me, leading me on, the voice urges, "Come on. There isn't much time. Hurry. Get up."

"I am up. I am a spaceman."

"That's impossible. There's no such thing. Follow me."

I follow the voice, past the stars and into the deep velvet ink of darkness. Somewhere, I notice the engine sound growing louder, and then it stops.

22

The rumbling of the truck jarred Paul out of sleep, but the rumbling persisted and never changed. He realized it was the pervasive and oddly foreign sound of an air conditioner. The second time Paul struggled out of the warmth of unconsciousness, he was more lucid and sure of his immediate past. He also felt comfortable. The anesthesia wearing off eased him back into a world he dimly remembered—but remembered nonetheless—leaving only short hours before. It was a world of mysteries and secrets, better left buried there in the haze of awakening. He vowed never to tell the chain of events that led him to this hospital, this bed, this truth that could not be and never would so long as he never spoke it. As long as things were left in the desert—unknown, consigned to the realm of lost mysteries and forgotten myths—Paul believed he might somehow return to a life that he remembered, a life that he could manage and believe.

He shifted in the hospital bed, which was soft and warm. He appreciated the large pillow that lay beneath his head. His body felt clean and dry. He relished the kind hum of air conditioning in the surrounding air. He could sense the presence of a stranger in the room with him, but he remembered everything that had brought him here. He knew who the stranger was, and he knew it was not Sergio. Not this time. He knew Sergio was dead. He knew that before he passed out from the fire in his gut. He remembered everything that had happened, and he swore he wouldn't repeat it to the stranger sitting in the chair at the foot of the bed. The stranger was a police officer with a notebook and a ready pen.

"I see you're awake," the cop said. Garcia, Paul remembered. That was his name.

Paul looked up at Garcia who stood from his chair and slowly walked towards the foot of Paul's bed. He was a short, thick-bodied and strong looking Mexican man with a trim black mustache and pleasant face. Sunlight pouring into the room illuminated him like an actor on a stage. He held his clipboard in a formal manner as he approached Paul, desperate to ask questions, questions, questions.

Paul's sight had come back only moments before he lost consciousness and the last things he saw, which in a way were the first, were burned into his mind. He would be able to draw the scene for the rest of his life. But it would be madness ever to tell.

A cave darker than anything I could describe—lightning and gunfire, an animal howling

Weary and weak, Paul hoped the young cop would let him just drift off to sleep. He closed his eyes, steadfastly ignoring the other man's presence until he was alone, floating through the bed and falling, falling...

When Paul woke again, darkness skirted the edges of the room; the shadows coming through the blinds had grown moody and tired. Paul looked around at every new sight with amazement, enjoying the new patterns created by the change in light. Even this barren and dingy white hospital room with the cheap plastic flowers—they were blue—looked beautiful to him. An old TV hung on a scratched metal platform, staring vacantly down at Paul. The handsome Mexican cop standing in the garish fluorescent light seemed a saint painted on a religious candle. Everything was a welcome sight. Paul smiled.

"I'm glad you're okay," Garcia said. "You lost some blood."

"Sergio is dead, isn't he?"

"Sergio?" Garcia asked. He squinted his eyes slightly and wrote the name down in his notepad. "Who is Sergio?" Garcia asked, looking up at Paul.

"Sergio Ramirez was my...captor." Paul felt ashamed to describe Sergio that way. "He got washed away in a flash flood."

"Sergio, huh? They found his body washed up on the Okracoke Ranch. Billy Staples called us up when he found it. That's where we started—figured it was connected with you and McCain somehow." Garcia paused and watched Paul for some kind of reaction. Paul just stared back. "Sergio," Garcia said, repeating the name, "that's what he told you his name was?"

Paul struggled to sit up. Pain shot through his side, and he looked down at the ugly black stitches holding his skin together. He groaned, but managed to sit up and face Garcia. "What do you mean? Joey? Yeah, that's his name."

"No, this other guy. He told you his name was Sergio?"

"His name *was* Sergio."

Garcia nodded and clucked his tongue. "We knew him as Eddie Teach. That's the name he was born with— Edward Teach. Real SOB he was."

"I don't understand."

"He changed his name quite a bit. Had some various troubles with the law, killed some folks back in the early seventies. Kept changing his name. Basically, they lost him until I stumbled on his picture in an old back file and remembered seeing him in a gas station a couple days ago. I did some digging. Sergio Ramirez… right." Garcia laughed darkly and shook his head. "Dark skin, but he was a white man. Eddie Teach was his name. Can't you tell a white man from a Mexican?"

"He told me he killed a truck driver who killed his family."

"Yeah. That's true. He killed a truck driver. Most folks figured he killed his own family though. And a few others. After the trucker there were a few unexplained murders around the southwest. Up here and down in old Mexico, Chihuahua, Juarez. I guess he invented this Sergio persona for himself and somehow managed to find a center or a balance or something. A way to live with himself and not have to kill no one else, you know?" Garcia shrugged. "He just retired."

"That's impossible. He was a good man."

Garcia laughed a grim cop laugh. "He got away with things most people would get put to sleep for."

Paul closed his eyes. His head felt as if it were swimming, like someone was pounding his temple with a sledgehammer. He chalked it up to the drugs. He couldn't understand how this could be. He wanted to cry for Sergio's death, Sergio who had saved his life. "Why didn't he kill me?"

"Eddie created new personalities for himself. He literally became other people. He'd probably been Sergio so long it was hard not to think as Sergio. He became this Sergio guy and went away to hide and got lost until he couldn't even find his way out of his own disguise." Garcia shook his head and looked directly at Paul. "Truth is I don't know why you're alive, but if I was you, I'd count myself extremely lucky."

"Are you going to arrest me?" Paul asked. He didn't care anymore. He stared up at the white paneled ceiling with its little black holes randomly punched in the panels like negative stars among nebulous brown stains from ancient air conditioner leaks.

"No. Why would we? It was self-defense, and the wife isn't pressing any charges."

"The wife? I don't understand. I heard I was wanted for killing some cop."

"Not some cop. A friend of mine. Harold." Garcia paused for a moment, seeming to collect his thoughts and let things settle a bit. He resumed, "It's clear that Joey McCain killed him. You got yourself stuck in between a family squabble."

"How do you know that?" Paul asked.

"He killed him, and when you came through that diner he saw a way to shift the blame from himself. He followed you out of town and ran you off the road. Into that boat, and then he figured you were dead—and I must say it's real hard to believe you aren't—and left the murder weapon on you."

"The murder weapon?"

"The gun you shot him with. That was his own gun. Poetic justice if you ask me," Garcia said through a smirk. "I don't like seeing any man die, but I'm not shedding tears for the guy who killed a buddy of mine."

"The lights," Paul whispered. "His truck was the lights."

"What lights?" Garcia asked.

"Nothing," Paul said, feeling only slightly more relieved. There was more, but if he could avoid it he would never tell Garcia.

"Anyways, lucky for you Eddie Teach finds you and takes you home. Takes the gun too. McCain has a run in with you and finds you're still alive so he sets out to kill you. He drove around out there in the desert for days. Meanwhile, you manage to get the gun away from Teach before he gets washed away just before McCain finally stumbles along and picks up your trail. You led him to that cave.

...the cave, I remember it, but it will be forgotten...

You guys fought. End of story. Thanks for visiting Armbister and we hope you come back." Garcia shook his head in respectful disbelief. "Man, talk about digging your own grave. You are one lucky SOB."

The lights weren't real. The lights weren't real.

Take a bunch of lights on a pickup truck, throw in a stout head injury and suddenly you have UFO sightings. In a way, Paul felt vindicated, but he also knew he was fully awake when he led Joey to that cave. He was also blind, a fact he was content not to bring up around Garcia. Let the cop think he could see the whole time. Paul knew he would spend years trying to understand how in hell he found that cave in the middle of the desert. Paul closed his eyes and smiled.

"Get some rest," Garcia said as he put his hat back on his head and walked towards the door. "We got some papers for you to fill out, mostly just a self-defense statement. It won't be disputed. After that, you're free to go, Mr. Reynolds."

Paul nodded. "How did you know to come looking for me? How did you find me?"

"McCain's wife called me up. Told me her man killed Officer Benson because he was sleeping with her and that her husband was going to kill you next. He figured out where you were staying. Probably wanted to ambush you, but you weren't there. He went hunting. His missus let me know where he was heading and what he aimed to do. He used to like to beat on her. I guess she isn't too disappointed either."

Paul lay in the bed for hours. The wound in his side throbbed with each breath but not so bad that he wanted to push the call button to bring the nurse with the morphine that would put him out of his misery. The doctors said it would hurt for a few days. The stitches would dissolve and the pain would slowly recede, but there was some nerve damage. He knew he would always feel the wound where the bullet went in and somehow missed all of his important organs before tearing an exit just inches from his spine.

Regardless of the dull pain in his side and the boredom of lying in a hospital bed while nurses observed and cops questioned him, he felt safer in the hospital than he ever did with Sergio.

Eddie.

He stared at the ceiling for a long time trying to remember everything Sergio had told him. Trying to square it with the story told by the Mexican cop with the neat mustache. He gave up. Beside the bed, a black remote control dangled from a thin silver chain that kept it nearby. Paul clicked the power button and watched the TV across the room blaze to bluish life. He hit the mute button and flipped through channels. He had no desire to hear it. He just wanted to watch it. To see it.

He studied each channel. Armbister didn't have very many, but each was a wonder of color like autumn leaves changing in the mountains. He watched old sitcoms and game shows and soap operas. American Movie Favorites was showing an old black and white film, some cinema classic. He passed it by in favor of seeing more color. The weather channel was his favorite. Big colorful maps with the shapes of sun throughout the southwest and rain in Louisiana and Washington and a big wavy line with small humps depicted a stationary warm front. Charts indicated with red bars that for two weeks, record high temperatures, exceeding 110 degrees on some days, had gripped the local area and broken only with the rain that had taken Sergio. Periodically, a beautiful black woman in a classy suit would come on and gesticulate at the changing maps and point to weather occurrences around the country. The map and the woman disappeared and were replaced by scenery from around the nation: wind-bent palm trees in Hawaii, snow-covered mountains in Colorado, and the inviting sand-bar coast of North Carolina.

Paul let go of the remote control, and it fell off the bed. The chain caught it before it could hit the floor, and it swung in mid-air. A squeak rose from the old bolt that held the chain to the hospital bed. He stared at the TV for a very long time and enjoyed the colorful graphics that showed mold indexes in red and green on a blue background. He marveled at the way the lovely weathercaster's gold earrings and thin gold necklace shone against her black skin. He fell asleep before the first commercial break, the searing pain in his side all but forgotten.

As he slept, Paul dreamed the events that had led from the arroyo and Sergio's death and finally to the cave. They took on nightmare proportions, often waking him in a terrified sweat. The third time he woke crying, and he forced himself to stay awake as long as he could to reset his dreaming mind and try to push it towards something more benign. It was dark outside. Someone had come into his room and turned off the TV and dimmed the lights so only a small red nightlight glowed dimly from inside the bathroom.

He wanted to forget what happened. To never repeat it and never remember it. He forced himself to think of other scenes from his life, but the hospital kept reminding him of Shan and in one version of the dream it turned out to be Shan who was killed and not Joey. Shan was Joey. In another version of the dream it was Sergio who shot Paul, except that in this version it clearly wasn't Sergio, but was actually Eddie Teach. The nightmares were compounded by the way Sergio looked in the dreams: a hulking man, with muscles and a large gut but no face. There were no eyes nor any other features on Sergio's blank mask-like face. Perhaps this is what bothered Paul the most. Nothing had been seen. It had been perceived and heard and occasionally touched, but in his dreams, everything turned to nightmare because the images had to be filled in by an overactive and frightened imagination.

He gave up on sleep and turned the TV back on. The Yankees were playing. Paul watched the game without much interest. He stared at the TV the rest of the night.

23

It was only a few days before Paul was released from the hospital. "Keep the wounds clean and be careful," the tall balding doctor said as he escorted Paul to the nurse's station where he was given back his wallet, which was all he had on him when the cops caught up with him at the cave. While filling out paperwork and handing over his credit card, Garcia walked up and stood next to him.

"What do you want?" Paul asked without looking up. "I can go, right?"

"Yeah."

"Where's the rest of my stuff?"

"Back at Teach's place, I suppose."

"I want it. Is it okay to go and get what's mine?"

Garcia laughed. "Hell, you can take it all for all I care."

Paul nodded and looked up at Garcia. Garcia held Paul's camera bag. It looked scratched and torn, but Paul's heart surged in his chest when he saw it. He pushed his release forms across the table to the young nurse sitting on the other side. She was too young to have her hair in such a severe bun, which gave her the look of an uptight schoolteacher. She tore away the white and pink copies, and slid the yellow, bottom copy, back to Paul.

"Have a nice day, Mr. Reynolds." She smiled sweetly at him.

"Thanks," he said moving away. Garcia stayed with him. He handed the camera bag to Paul. "I don't know how to get there. I don't know where he lived," Paul said as he dug through the bag looking over his equipment in the quiet white-tiled hallway of the small hospital.

"You must of known the area pretty good to have found that cave."

The cameras were beaten and the backs hung open. Some local one-hour processor had developed all the film, and the pictures were all sitting in grocery store envelopes. Paul thumbed through the pictures, disappointed to see the bluish cast that indicated his beautiful black and white pictures had been spoiled by having been developed in a color process. Paul next examined one of the cracked lenses. He shook his head as he put down the ruined lens and picked up the body of his camera. He pushed the release; to his joy, it clicked and the motor drive whirred dutifully. New lenses, and all might be well, Paul thought. He looked back up at Garcia. Even with much of his gear busted, he still felt good having it back.

"I don't know how I found it," Paul said remembering Garcia's question. "Just stumbled on it. I don't even know how I got to the house, Sergio—Eddie—brought me while I was out cold. He fixed me up. Said he was a medic in Vietnam." Paul spoke the last almost as a question.

Garcia nodded. "Yeah, he had a service record. Honorable discharge even. Sergeant Teach. I think he must of been one of them that came home without all his pieces put together right."

"I guess so."

Garcia removed a piece of paper from his clipboard and drew a crude map. He marked Armbister and the main drag out of town. "Here you get off the road," he said. "Take the dirt road—it's marked pretty good—and follow it about five miles. You'll see it."

Paul nodded and took the piece of paper. He looked at it, then folded it up and stuffed it into his shirt pocket, taking a moment to notice the faded blue of the old button-down shirt. It was just an ordinary blue, except that it was a color he hadn't noticed yet since waking up. It was the exact blue of an autumn sky in Nevada he saw two years earlier. Paul eventually looked up at Garcia who was giving him a curious look.

"You sure you're okay?" Garcia asked.

"Yeah—oh, hey, is there an observatory around here?" Paul asked. "A small private one," he added.

"Yeah. Keep going down that main highway about ten miles, then go left on county 19105. It loops back about eight or ten miles. Old house with a big dome on the roof. No one lives there. Why?"

"No one?"

"Not since the old man died about ten years back. He was a crazy old bird too. Why?"

Paul blinked in confusion, shaking his head. "I… I was curious, I guess. I saw it once and wanted to take a closer look."

Garcia smiled knowingly and looked at Paul. "That's where you were heading isn't it?"

"No. I was going to the east coast. I've never seen that part of the country."

"Me either. I'm from El Paso." Garcia extended his hand. "Sorry you got caught up in all this mess. Armbister is a nice town. Good people." Garcia looked down at his feet, searching for words to express an awkward curiosity. "We looked at your film," he said. "You're a good photographer." Garcia watched Paul's expression change from passive to guilty and a bit hurt. "I guess that's like reading your diary or something."

Paul nodded. "I like to process my own film."

"We were just trying to look for a reason you didn't come to us when you knew you were wanted. After you saw the TV news at Ernie's."

"Right," was all Paul could think to say. Garcia had seen the UFO Frisbee pictures. Paul looked away.

"You ever been abducted?" Garcia whispered.

"No."

"Well, besides by Teach, I guess."

"Yeah—No—I don't really think he abducted me. I think he saved my life."

"You're a lucky son of a bitch. By rights one or the other of them should have killed you."

"I guess I am," Paul muttered as he shouldered his camera bag and strode away from Garcia.

"By the way, you still have to appear in court to let them know how you're going to take care of the ticket," Garcia called after him.

Paul turned and stared. "My ticket?"

"You were speeding."

Paul nodded. "I'll send a check."

Garcia smiled. "I'm sure you will."

24

Paul stepped out of the hospital into the blinding desert sun. He stood outside the door for a long time holding his hand over his eyes to shade them. When they adjusted, he could see Armbister's main street spread out before him. Feed stores and pickup trucks and not much else. Most of the buildings contained spaces that were once thriving businesses, but now were not much more than relics. Armbister was another town drying up as the dreams of the young led them to other destinies until all that was left were the older folks, waiting patiently for the desert to come and sweep them away. Paul noticed two patrol cars parked at the police station across the street from the small hospital. In the distance, he saw Ernie's Joint.

"Paul," a woman shouted from the street. "Paul Reynolds!"

Paul looked around and found the source of the unfamiliar voice. A leggy blonde woman leaned against a red Acura smoking a cigarette. She looked like a misplaced model. She called his name again and waved her hand at him, a silver bracelet catching the sunlight.

"What?" Paul yelled back, wondering where or if he had ever seen her before.

The woman tossed the butt of her cigarette on the ground and walked towards him. Paul watched her approach. She wore tight, short cut-off jeans and a thin white t-shirt. Paul admired her figure until she was standing next to him and pulling him towards her car. He looked at the well-hidden wrinkles on her face. The wrinkles spoke of years that her body did not show.

"Name's KC," she said. "KC McCain? You killed my husband."

Paul pulled away from her. "He was trying to kill me." Paul watched her face. "I'm sorry," he mumbled.

"I know, I know. Lousy son of a bitch got every bit he deserved. I feel bad about you getting all caught up in this on account of me. He killed Harold 'cause I was screwing him you know, but I feel bad so I want to give you his truck. I don't need it, but I want you to come with me. You can shower and clean up and take his truck, 'cause I don't need it, and I don't want to look at the damn thing no more." KC spoke breathlessly as she herded Paul towards the car and opened the door and gently pushed him into the passenger seat. The interior was spotless; it even had the vague vanilla smell of a new car. KC hurried around behind the car and got in. She fastened her seatbelt and looked over at Paul.

"Seat belt," she said before starting the engine.

Paul buckled his belt and looked at her as she pulled away from the hospital and pressed on the gas. Soon they were tearing down the highway at close to a hundred. I'll never drive too fast again, Paul thought.

Once they were going, KC looked Paul over and smiled. "He was a real bastard. You did me a big favor."

"I was protecting myself. It was self-defense."

"I know," KC said. "Now, I did say you could have his truck, but I want something from you."

"What?"

"What in the hell happened? Joey told me you were blind. How in hell did you kill him? I read about it in the weekly. It didn't sound like no blind man shot him in self-defense."

"I don't want to talk about it. You wouldn't believe it so there's no point."

"Try me. Officer Garcia showed me them UFO pictures you took—him and me go way back—so I know you got a pretty crazy story and—"

"Those pictures are fake," Paul cut her off.

"They sure don't look like they're fakes to me."

Paul smiled in spite of himself. "Trust me."

"Okay, they're fake. So what? How did you find the cave and kill Joey? You tell me, and I give you his truck. Otherwise, I let you out here, and it's a hell of a long walk back to town."

Paul bristled. He didn't want to talk about caves and fights and impossible solutions to hopeless problems. He didn't want solutions that couldn't be real because then he couldn't be real, and then what was anything supposed to mean? He stared out the window at the miles of sameness that looked exactly as they always had. The scenery, outside his mind at least, never changed. It was the internal scenery that worried Paul.

She pulled the car off the road and into a decrepit trailer park. All the trailers looked old and beaten down except for one, which Paul guessed would surely be hers. She stopped the car in front of the clean white trailer with the cactus garden out front. Next to it stood a large blue dually pickup truck. Paul recognized it from the parking lot at Ernie's, and he knew he would recognize the fog lights and deer lights from the crazy dreams.

KC stared at Paul.

"Tell me, please. Tell me the truth." Her pleading eyes locked Paul's. For whatever reason, she wanted to know everything as if it would somehow make a difference to her, as if somehow it would change her feelings about losing her man, son of a bitch though she claimed he was. Her gaze made Paul uncomfortable, and he looked away. When he looked back, her eyes begged, and he watched her fight tears. She was hard, but according to her eyes, part of her must have loved him at one time and that part needed closure. She needed to know what and how it happened. Besides, even with his sight, Paul had no intention of hiking back to town. He looked at her, watched her face, and finally spoke.

Canis ex Machina

This sounds crazy, and I don't blame you for a second if you don't believe it.

I'm not sure I believe it myself, but I can't imagine how I could be alive or even where that cop said he found me if it wasn't true. I wanted to believe maybe I had dreamed it all, lying in a hospital bed, comatose, after a bad motorcycle crash. Or maybe I just somehow sleepwalked to the cave or something. Just dreaming the whole way. Maybe Sergio Ramirez never existed.

I believe he did, though.

I have to believe it. It makes no sense, but I have to believe because I can find no other way to continue.

I wandered around alone, probably just in circles. It was odd too, because the whole time I was walking I heard footsteps or breathing, right next to me, but there was never anyone there. I just figured I was hallucinating. Eventually I just gave up. I sat for a long time, and I guess I just passed out or went to sleep.

When I woke, there was this engine driving nearby, so I fired the gun to attract attention, but pretty soon, there were shots coming right at me. So I ran, just desperate to get away, you know like fight or flight? I chose flight. I didn't run long before I fell on a rock. I guess I passed out. I dreamt of the crash as I had been for the past few days. Sometimes there was this voice that talked to me. This time it kept urging me, 'Come on. Come on. Hurry up.' Like that. It warned me to wake up and hurry. It didn't say why or where. Just hurry. Finally, I wake up and I'm still there holding that damn gun which wasn't even Sergio's—he didn't have it till he found me—and I'm just lying there, right.

When I'm fully awake, I still hear the voice.

"Come on. Get up. Hurry. Follow me."

Stuff like that. I try to shake it off, figuring it's just my imagination, but this voice is actually inside my head. Like a separate presence and not just me thinking in a different voice, you know how you argue with yourself? It wasn't like that. It was urgent.

I stood and felt that the sky was starting to warm up, and that the sun was on its way, so I knew I had slept through the night, and I felt recharged. I listened to the desert for a long time, and I felt naked and really like a sitting duck because for all I knew there was a mountain lion or something waiting to get me. Or that the guy with the gun was just watching me.

And the voice starts telling me to dance.

I tried to ignore it.

"Dance."

It seemed the most ridiculous thing.

"Dance. Dance. Dance," it said.

I couldn't fight it. It was like it was overpowering my thoughts and there was nothing I could do. It was louder than my thoughts. So I did a stupid little jig, and it just kept goading me on. "Dance."

So I danced, and as the sun came up and it started to warm me and dry the dew out of my clothes, I danced harder and harder, and as I danced it was like I was surrendering control of myself because I laughed at myself and I—I cried, for Sergio, and I kept dancing and the more I hurt or laughed or cried, the harder I danced, and then something extraordinary happened.

I saw.

I saw in black and white and just in quick flashes like fast cuts in a music video or something, but I saw.

I saw myself.

Every image was a quick glance at myself from a few feet away and low down near the ground. I saw myself, dirty and wet and covered in blood, holding a gun and dancing hard, flailing around like a lunatic, really, like I was slam-dancing without music and behind me the sun beginning to break the horizon, and all about me was desert and dark mountains.

I wanted to stop and stare through these alien eyes and for the first time really see myself, but the voice told me to dance while these flickering images of myself kept racing through my mind.

This had happened to me once earlier, and I realized what was the same.

I stopped dancing. I stopped moving, and the blackness washed over me. The images stopped.

I waited and listened and said:

"Mercury?"—That was Sergio's dog. He said she was part coyote too. Anyways, she barked, and as she barked the voice in my head said:

"I'm right here."

I stood there like an idiot while the voice laughed. Another image of myself shot into my head, this time looking up at my face as if from my feet. I reached down and found Mercury's head. Her eyes, of course, were exactly where the camera that was sending me these images should have been.

She licked my hand.

"Come on," the voice urged—the voice from my dreams. The voice that went with that bark, but she wasn't barking this time. There was just the wind and that voice shimmering like golden light in my head.

"I don't believe it," I said.

The voice just laughed again.

"Hurry. He's coming. He heard the gunshots. He's looking."

"Sergio?"

There was a long pause, and I heard a long and pitiful howl in my head, but no sound my ears could hear. "No," the voice said. "The other one. And there are gray men with hats behind him, but they won't find you first."

"What can I do?" I asked. I couldn't believe I was actually talking to a dog, but at this point I decided I had completely lost my mind so I should just run with whatever chances presented themselves. I knew I was pretty well screwed if I just waited, and I was certain 'the other one' would be Joey coming to shoot me.

"He will follow you," Mercury said. "Let him. He is hurt; the blood is running out of his body. You must make his heart pump faster."

"Hurt?"

"He was bitten while looking around Sergio's home yesterday."

"You?"

The voice just laughed.

"Where are we going?"

"Hold my neck," she said.

I bent down and took hold of the loose skin around her neck —the puppy handle, you know? I held it and just started walking next to her. She trotted pretty fast, and I struggled to keep up. I was scared I was going to fall over something or nail a cactus, but every time something came up, she shot me a picture of the landscape, and I knew where to walk to avoid hitting it.

"He's coming," she said. "There's a cave."

We made for the base of a nearby mountain ridge, and after about an hour or so of walking, we were there. Every now and again, I could hear the engine of his truck roaring over the desert in crazed patterns, hunting aimlessly before it would stop and then start again as if he was looking for us and stopping from time to time to search.

Eventually, we made it to a cave and she led me inside.

"Safe here," her voice said in my head.

I asked her if all of them could talk.

She asked me if all of us were deaf.

She led me to the back of the cave and told me to wait and then she left me.

It wasn't long before Joey made it to the cave. Mercury yipped and hollered from outside, her voice growing fainter as she scurried away. Then, I could hear him breathing. It sounded real rough, like he was tired and hurt, so I figured Mercury must have torn a good chunk out of him and that he must just be running on anger by this point.

He yelled into the cave, "I know you're in here! You pissed off some momma coyote. She's out there carrying on." I knew the voice from the gas station. It was Joey.

I just waited. His voice sounded like he was having trouble breathing, and I really thought he might collapse at any moment but he started into the cave. His footsteps were coming closer like he knew right where I was.

I heard Mercury growl and then bark and then a gunshot.

I heard Joey fall, he must have lost his balance and stumbled over something shooting at Mercury. The kick from the gun or something.

I got stupid and stood up, and he fired again and he hit me, right here in the side. The pain was like fire or electricity burning through my whole side, all the way in and out my back, like I got hit by lightning or something.

But I didn't care because I saw the muzzle flash. I saw it. It was bluish… like an electric spark.

I fell back, clutching my side and staring up at the ceiling. I saw it by the light from the entrance to the cave, which was real dim, but I could see the stalagmites or stalactites—the ones that hang down, whichever they are—and the shadows blazing across them. They were reddish brown, and I don't think I've ever seen anything so beautiful. I knew I could die, but I didn't care. I was just relieved to be able to see.

I was lying there, paying more attention to the ceiling of the cave than to my wound or anything else for that matter, and I heard Joey starting to stand. As he did, I saw his head and chest, but I don't think he saw me. I don't think his eyes were adjusted to the dark yet, but I could see perfectly. I was used to the dark. I had been living in it for days. I lifted my gun and fired. I never shot anybody before, but I didn't know what else to do.

He fell, and I lay there listening to his breathing and wondering if he was listening to mine. I guess we were both wondering whose would stop first.

His stopped not long before the cops showed up. They helped me out and took me to the hospital.

I was worried that Joey had shot Mercury, but on the way out I didn't see her. I looked, but she wasn't there. I wanted to look at her. I guess to thank her or something or maybe just know that she was alive, but the thing is I know she is. I know she always will be.

I don't think she can die.

25

"That's what happened," Paul said as he finished his story. He didn't expect he would ever tell anyone else, and he certainly didn't know what it meant or if it even meant anything, but part of him believed she had a right to know. Maybe I'm just tired of lying, he thought. And even if he was now stuck—stuck like a fly under glass—with a truth that sounded like a lie, he decided he would have to learn to be stuck with it because it was now his.

KC stared at Paul for a long time. The sun was low in the sky, and the desert shadows had grown long and raked across the old trailers like strange fingers. KC lit a cigarette and offered the pack to Paul. He declined. KC smiled. "I guess you only like to smoke weed?"

"How do you know?"

KC smiled. "That's all Joey took off you was your weed. It was pretty good."

"You still have any?"

"No. It's gone. Lucky for you he took that before the cops found your stuff. They go hard on people for that around here." She smiled and said quietly, "A few of them anyway."

Paul nodded. It didn't matter.

"You know, I was going to invite you in and ask if you wanted to make love to me. I want to be a mama, but Joey could never quite deliver the goods. I don't need a man; I want a kid though. So I mostly screwed around with cops thinking they have to pass certain tests, physical fitness and the like so they must have good genes. But when I got to know certain guys they had traits and things I didn't like. I saw you and thought you and me we could make a good baby, but I listen to you, and you're a nut farmer."

"I told you the truth. I didn't lie about any of that."

"I know. I know. It ain't a lie if you believe it yourself."

"I'm not crazy. I didn't invent this stuff."

"Look, I appreciate the honesty and all. I mean what should I expect from a guy with pictures full of flying saucers and stuff. So I'm still going to give you Joey's truck and whatever else you want of his 'cause it's his fault you lost your bike so I guess that's just the decent thing to do. But that's all." She stared at Paul, looked him up and down and shrugged. "I guess you can have a shower too."

A few hours and a hot shower later, Paul and KC stood under the garish yellow bug light that illuminated her front porch. June bugs buzzed just outside the circle of light and occasionally one bounced against the side of the white trailer.

KC handed Paul the keys to Joey's truck. Paul stuffed them in his pocket and then helped her load her little red car with the suitcases she told him she had packed while he was in the hospital. "I was just waiting for you," she said as she slammed the back door of her car.

"Where are you going to go?" Paul asked.

"I'm moving towards Amarillo. I always wanted to live in the big city, and I'll be a little closer to my sister there." She looked around her. "I hate this little shithole town. Nothing happens here. They don't even have any postcards. All the ones they sell at the gas station are pictures of other places."

Paul nodded. "I really haven't seen much around here."

"Believe me, there ain't nothing to see." KC smiled and settled into her car and rolled down the window. "Thank you, Paul," she said. KC rolled up the window, pointed the car towards Amarillo and disappeared into the moonless night.

26

Paul watched the sun rise from the infinity of Sergio's desert front yard. He stared in wonder at the mountains and the many silent plants that had been invisible a few days before, but that now held Paul's fascination as much as anything else. He imagined Sergio standing out here, morning after morning, a twisted king of heat and time.

The man just wasn't an Eddie Teach. He was Sergio, huge and faceless, and always would be in Paul's memory. The house was tiny, built of old cracked adobe and a wooden roof daubed with mud. Pieces of the house had begun to cave in, and to finally see it, Paul was amazed it even still stood. Pieces of the wood seemed to be rotting, and Paul wondered if Sergio ever intended to fix anything or would the house have just fallen into decay as its master aged. Sergio's weathered yellow truck, wearing a million old battle scars sat near the fire pit, a ring of black-singed rock surrounding a piece of burned earth.

Old logs lay scattered about and a face, half-carved on one of them, stared vacantly up at Paul. He recognized his own face, dirty and bearded and scratched. The face had no eyes. Paul wondered if Sergio ever had any intention of putting eyes on the face. It reminded Paul of a death mask, and he shuddered as he recalled Garcia's words about being incredibly lucky to be alive. There were other faces including an old woman that Paul decided would be Sary. All the faces were lined up against one side of the house. He stared at each in turn, admiring their artistry and wondering what stories went with each one; he wondered if they had been family, friends, or victims. Scattered among them, Paul saw Jesuses and MacArthurs. He noticed nothing special with his eyes, and wondered if the magic of these wooden faces would always be locked away in what his fingers were able to see.

Paul stepped inside. Dim light shrouded the house almost as effectively as blindness, and minutes passed before Paul's eyes fully adjusted to the dusky gloom. Paul looked at the old couch he had awakened on and the carefully handmade coffee table in front of it. He glanced at the rugged shelf and the mismatched cabinets scavenged from who knew where. The place was crushingly small, not the forbidding infinite space that Paul had drifted in for fearful days. Amazement filled him when he remembered that he had once been lost inside this little room.

A dirty sheet served as a curtain between the living area and the bedroom. Paul pushed the curtain aside and stepped through to Sergio's bedroom. There was nothing more than an old mattress lying on the floor with three colorful Mexican border town blankets strewn across it. Paul desperately wanted to know what Sergio looked like. Perhaps if he found an image to fix in his mind, he could ease his dreams by replacing the faceless demon with a human, a real man who had helped him. He searched every drawer and cabinet, finding only old silverware and an assortment of camping supplies.

Finally, lost in shadows on the bottom shelf of a crude bookcase that contained an esoteric collection of biographies and mythologies, Paul stumbled on a pair of old and worn photographs. One showed a young homely looking Mexican woman holding a baby boy whose tight curly black hair spilled out around his face. The baby was laughing, and the woman—could it be Elena?—looked at the camera, a nervous smile frozen across her plain features.

The other photograph revealed a pair of young soldiers standing in the jungle, smiling proudly at the camera. One of the men was big and dark with curly black hair and a scraggly beard, the kind grown by young men trying to appear older. His piercing blue eyes seemed to stare at Paul through the sheet of photo paper and across the magnificent desert of time that separated them. He wore sergeant's stripes on his uniform and held a machine gun, but no medical bag. He looked very much like the baby in the other picture.

Paul stared at the baby and the bearded man. Father and son. Paul put the pictures back on the shelf and walked outside. He knew what Eddie Teach looked like. He had a mental picture, and he tried to put a lifetime of hardscrabble living along with an extra hundred pounds on him, but he couldn't. He couldn't adjust the picture to fit what he knew.

He looked at the faces against the house, now picking out Elena and the boy, both long dead whether at the hand of a drunken trucker or the one man they surely counted on, Paul would never know, but he chose the story Sergio had given him because revenge made more sense than sporadic episodes of madness. At least he believed he could understand that because along with revenge came redemption, unlike madness from which Paul saw no escape.

Paul picked up the log that bore the carving of his own face, and tossed it into the bed of the pickup truck. He brought all of his possessions out of the house and put them into Joey's pickup as well. When he loaded the truck with his things and a few of the more interesting books including an old biographical work about the great pirates, a worn hard-cover book of coyote legends, and an outdated guidebook about the wildlife of the Southwest, Paul went back to the bookcase and pulled the pictures out again. He stared at them for a long time until he realized he was looking at a picture of Edward Teach and not one of Sergio. Teach died long before Sergio was born, and Paul doubted he would ever know exactly what Sergio Ramirez had looked like. He left the pictures on the shelf and walked outside into the glaring sun.

He called for Mercury. He knew she wouldn't come, but he waited anyway. He would spend the rest of his life pondering how and why she had led him to the cave and saved his life. He knew the new life he had been given would never be what the old one was. He had been given answers to questions he never asked, and the answers begged greater questions. He would carry forever the burden of a riddle for which there could never be an answer. A question that he could never ask another person to solve. A story no thinking person would ever accept as truth. And yet, there it was. To him everything seemed crystal clear.

He glanced around at Sergio's old adobe hut one last time and scanned the horizon in case Mercury should return, but she was gone, and he knew it. Still, he waited for two hours before he finally gave up and started the truck's smooth and powerful engine, so different from the old dying engine of Sergio's truck that was now abandoned, along with the hut and all that it contained, to the eternal wind and dust and sun of the eroding desert until it would be claimed by nature and left as misunderstood relics of time forgotten.

He drove back to the main road.

27

Dr. Jakes's observatory was really nothing more than a small wooden house nestled near the top of a very steep hill, a far cry from the great mountaintop dome Paul had imagined. It did have a domed roof, though. Paul looked up the rickety old steps with no rail that led to the door. The sun was low on the horizon when he began the long ascent. He walked slowly up the precipitous steps, the whole while being careful not to look down. Paul saw that the climb would be near impossible without the steps, and he wondered if the old doctor was even capable of the climb at all. The observatory reminded Paul of an Anasazi cliff dwelling, impossible and ancient and full of mystery, so precariously did it cling to the edge of the hill. His wound burned with the exertion of the climb, and he had to stop periodically and let it cool.

When Paul reached the top, he could see the desert spread out before him for dozens of miles in every direction. The sun slipped below the horizon, and far to the west the diamond twinkling starlight of Armbister began on the desert floor. The sky turned indigo, then deep black as Paul watched the summer stars come out one by one. Outshining them all was Arcturus, followed by Vega, bright star of Lyra, high on the Meridian, and Paul mused that perhaps, in Dr. Jakes's mind, these two were the only stars left.

Paul watched night engulf the desert from his high eagle's perch and wondered what strange tug of unknown gravities brought him to this place outside Jakes's door. Perhaps, he just wanted to *see* images on the photo plates Jakes had talked about. Perhaps it was just to see Jakes, to hold onto some connection with the things he had experienced on the dark planet with the radio sun. Maybe it was to know that Jakes, at least, really existed in the reassuringly familiar wavelengths of visible light. And part of him, he realized, was there just to make sure the old man would get on all right without Sergio and not be forgotten, consigned to oblivion with all the other old myths and legends of the desert sands.

Paul's mind drifted back to Garcia and his skeptic's claim that the old man had died long before. Paul paused, afraid that Garcia might be right. But he knew the old man existed. He believed in him, and he knew that on the other side of the door, the old man would be waiting and would welcome him into his home.

He turned and knocked on the wooden door. His knocks didn't make the door rattle in its frame the way Sergio's had, loud and delicate and full of tonal nuances, but the view was good, and he was happy to be able to see the desert and mountains stretching off in every direction. He was happy to see the light paint delicate colors on the clouds as it failed. He was happy to once again see the stars.

About the Author

James Brush lives in Austin, TX where he writes, teaches high school English, and watches birds. You can find him online at *Coyote Mercury* and Twitter (@jdbrush).

Also by James Brush:

Birds Nobody Loves

www.ingramcontent.com/pod-product-compliance
Lightning Source LLC
Chambersburg PA
CBHW020302200626
46814CB00006BA/2048